D1569162

WAY OF THE LAWLESS

Joe Peters and his partner Butch Shilton have been on the run for a year. On their way to prison for shooting a cheating gambler, a gang of outlaws murdered their escort — a crime for which the pair have been blamed. Trouble follows them everywhere, and they end up in the brutal Los Pecos penitentiary. Breaking out, they flee to Mexico, only to fall foul of the notorious bandit Barca. With enemies closing in on all sides, could this be the end of the trail for Butch and Joe?

P. McCORMAC

WAY OF THE LAWLESS

Complete and Unabridged

LINFORD
Leicester

First published in Great Britain in 2017 by
Robert Hale
an imprint of The Crowood Press
Wiltshire

First Linford Edition
published 2019
by arrangement with
The Crowood Press
Wiltshire

A catalogue record for this book is available
from the British Library.

ISBN 978–1–4448–4274–6

Published by
F. A. Thorpe (Publishing)
Anstey, Leicestershire

Set by Words & Graphics Ltd.
Anstey, Leicestershire
Printed and bound in Great Britain by
T. J. International Ltd., Padstow, Cornwall

This book is printed on acid-free paper

For John Auerbach and Joe Gilbert

1

'Butch, can you hear something?'

'Sure, when I lean my head on your breast I can hear the beating of your heart.'

'No, silly. I thought I heard a noise. Like someone moving around.'

'Huh, maybe a rat.'

A voice came out of the dark, loud and accusing:

'It ain't no rat, unless you're talking about yourself.'

'Father?'

'Arrest that serpent, Sheriff.'

A match flared in the dark as a lantern was ignited. Its light revealed a man and woman scrambling to their feet, dusting straw from their clothing.

'Evening, Reverend. No need to get all riled up.' The speaker grabbed a hat from a peg. A gunbelt hung from the same peg. 'We were just sitting here in

1

the dark, talking. People like privacy from time to time, and seeing as you banned me from your parlour I had no option but to meet Josephine in a quiet place like this. If I took her to my hotel room that would surely not have met with your approval. What's a man to do, I ask you?'

'Fella, shut your mouth.'

A second figure loomed beside the preacher. The man who had lured the preacher's daughter, Josephine, into the livery stables, saw the gleam of a star on the man's waistcoat. Sheriff Stanley Richards was of stocky build with blunt features. Not only did the light from the lamp reflect from the star, it also gleamed dully on a Colt .45 in the sheriff's hand.

'I'm taking you down the hoosegow.' There was a leer on the sheriff's face as he held the man at gunpoint. 'I've been going through some Wanted posters. Butch Shilton, wanted for murder. There's more, but you know already all the crimes you're guilty of.'

'Butch!' The girl was staring wide-eyed at her companion. 'Is this true?'

'Josephine, I swear to you I was framed. Judge Parsons had a particular grudge against me. He made up a pile of false charges and sentenced me to ten years in the pen. I never killed no lawmen. It was a gang of outlaws as jumped us and murdered that sheriff and his deputy and I got the blame for that.'

'Oh, thou false-hearted man, for your tongue is like a sharp razor working deceitfully,' Reverend Dinwiddie intoned. 'Please Lord, deliver us from evil men, for the mouth of the wicked, and the mouth of the deceitful are opened against me.

'Come away, my child. I will take you home and we will pray to God for your forgiveness. This vile creature has lured you from the paths of godliness. I thank the Lord we were in time to save you from this depraved monster.'

'Hang on, Reverend Dinwiddie, Josephine is pure as new-fallen snow and I was hoping some of her righteousness would rub off on me.'

'Humph,' Sheriff Richards grunted. 'You're right, Reverend, this fella has the forked tongue of a serpent, sure enough. The best place for him is behind bars where he can't do no more sinning and robbing and murdering and tempting young girls to sin with him.'

'Sheriff, I ain't like that, at all. Dang me, a fella has to put down roots somewhere, and I was figuring on settling in this here peaceable fine town of yours. But if all you can do is accuse me of crimes I did not commit then I will have no option but to shift my prospects on to someplace else.'

'Well, you can shift your prospects into a cage of iron bars. You're going to prison, Shilton, and I'm the man as is going to put you there.'

'Come, Josephine.'

The Reverend Dinwiddie held out his hand to his daughter. She cast a forlorn glance at Butch. His face was a study in injured innocence. Reverend Dinwiddie stepped forward to retrieve his daughter from the sinful influence of Butch and inadvertently moved in front of Sheriff Richards, leaving his gun unsighted. It was enough of an opportunity for Butch to make his play.

He tossed his hat into the preacher's face. Reverend Dinwiddie flinched and jerked back just as the sheriff was trying to edge round him to keep his gun sighted.

'Damnit!' the sheriff swore as the preacher stepped on his foot.

Butch dodged between the two men, hooked an arm around the lawman's neck and clamped his other hand on the gun. Josephine gasped and stepped back against the wall. Reverend Dinwiddie moved back also, staring apprehensively at the struggling men as they thrashed about, each trying to overturn the other.

'Damn you, Shilton!' the sheriff grunted. 'You'll hang for this. You ain't staying in no prison cell. It'll be a rope necktie for you.'

Butch said nothing, concentrating all his efforts in overpowering the sheriff. Their boots stomped in the dirt floor as they wrestled.

Reverend Dinwiddie watched anxiously as the men struggled.

'Give me a hand there, Reverend,' Sheriff Richards yelled.

Reverend Dinwiddie stepped closer to the men and pulled Butch's arm. He might as well have tugged at one of the uprights that held up the roof of the livery. Realizing how ineffectual his efforts were, the preacher let go and looked round for a weapon. The only thing of any use was a feed bucket. Quickly he picked it up and swung it at Butch.

'Yeoow!' Butch howled as the bucket hit him on the side of the head. He jerked to one side, lost his footing and both men hit the dirt with a thud. They broke apart.

Reverend Dinwiddie was enjoying himself. The last time he had hit anyone was when he chased two small boys and cuffed their ears for using strong language. As Sheriff Richards rolled to one side and lined up his Colt on the wanted man, the preacher lashed out at Butch with his improvised weapon. Once more, the preacher saved Butch as he stepped into the sheriff's line of fire.

'Goddamn it, Dinwiddie! Get out of the way. I'm going to blast that killer.'

Butch saw the bucket swinging towards him; swiftly he kicked the preacher's legs. Reverend Dinwiddie went down with a yell and let go the bucket. Butch fielded it and, seeing the sheriff aiming his Colt, slung it at the gun just as Sheriff Richards pulled the trigger.

The sheriff jerked aside as the bucket hit him. The shot intended for the wanted man embedded itself in the stable wall, showering Butch with splinters. Butch was on his feet now; in a few quick strides he reached the sheriff and kicked him in the face.

Sheriff Richards went over backwards. He was yelling incoherently, blood streaming from his mouth. He yelled some more when his attacker stood on his gun hand. His words were somewhat mangled for Butch's kick had broken his jaw.

Butch stooped and retrieved the Colt. Swiftly he stepped to where his own weapon was hanging on its peg. He turned to the young woman who was huddled against the back wall, staring at him with wide-eyed concern. Her father was lying on his back, his hands clasped together as he prayed fervently for deliverance from this fiend who, he believed, was about to murder them all.

'Goodbye Josephine,' Butch said, genuine regret in his voice. 'I sure wish we could have spent more time together.'

He turned and ran from the livery. Josephine raised a hand as if to wave goodbye but Butch was gone.

2

Joe Peters was a big man who liked nothing better than to sit at a well-laden table and tuck into some home-made fare. He had finished doing just that in Maud Ellison's diner and was contemplating moseying down to the Golden Horseshoe for an evening of card-playing. Maud, a widow three times over, had warmed to the big man since he had arrived in town and taken to having his meals at her diner.

The highlight of Joe's day was dinner. Usually he came away from this meal having made a glutton of himself with the main course and two or three helpings of delicious desserts. Tonight was no exception and Joe felt pleasantly bloated as he stood up from the table.

'Maud, if I stay in this town much longer I'll become too big to get through your front door. You must be the best cook in the whole of New Mexico.'

'I like to see a man eat,' the widow said coquettishly. 'The sight of a clean plate after a man's ate one of my meals is as good as a hymn of praise. It sure gives me satisfaction to see you tuck in. A real man needs proper food to keep him healthy.'

Joe, along with his partner, Butch Shilton, was on the run and had been for the last year after an unfortunate incident during a card game in which he had killed a cheating gambler. Joe had been sentenced to ten years in the state penitentiary.

He and Butch Shilton had been on the way to prison, when they encountered a gang of outlaws. The lawmen escorting the prisoners were murdered. Joe and Butch were blamed for the killing even though they had subsequently pursued the gang responsible for the murders and wiped them out.

Strangers up to that point, Joe and Butch had become friends and now they drifted, not staying in any place too long in case they came to the attention of the law.

As he wandered down to the Golden Horseshoe Joe was fantasizing about the well-endowed Maud.

'Sure is a fine-looking woman,' he opined out loud and belched contentedly. 'A man could do worse than settle down in this here town with a well set-up widow.'

It was a pleasant reverie and Joe arrived at the saloon more than convinced that he would be very happy to settle down with the widow and spend the rest of his life living in a gourmet's paradise.

But Joe wasn't sure if his daydream was unrealistic: perhaps he was deluding himself. He and Butch were on Wanted posters; one day someone would cotton on to who he was, and his dream of setting down would come to a violent end.

Dead or alive had an ominously fatal ring to it. Bounty hunters abounded and if they came after him there was a good chance that Maud Ellison would become a widow for a fourth time.

'Maybe it's time to move on,' he muttered and pushed inside the saloon for a night's gambling. Just as he stepped inside he thought he heard the faint sound of a gunshot. He paused for a moment, listening, his senses heightened by months of living on nerves attuned to every nuance of danger.

'Some drunken cowboy letting off steam, I reckon.'

There was a card school in progress and Joe stood watching.

'You gonna join us, Joe?'

'Reckon I will. Time I won some of my money back from you card-sharps.'

There was a murmur of nervous laughter from the players. Joe took a vacant chair and watched the cards being dealt. He heard someone come up behind him but paid it no attention. A hard round object pressed against the bone behind his ear. Joe went very still.

'Joe Peters, this is a gun I got shoved

against your skull. Deputy Hoskins is backing me with a shotgun. We got a Wanted poster with your name on it. It says dead or alive. It don't matter to me neither way. So if you want to live, place your hands flat on the table real careful like.'

Joe did as he was ordered. He realized now why the gamblers at the table had seemed nervous. They must have been in on the plan to arrest him. Right now they were scrambling to get away from the card table, leaving Joe all alone with the two armed deputies.

'In case you're wondering about your pal, Butch Shilton, Sheriff Richards is looking after him. About right now he should be taking that galoot to the jail. You going to come quiet?'

'I'll come quiet,' Joe said.

Other than committing suicide by putting up a fight, he could see no other option.

3

Butch Shilton was hastily saddling up the horses. As a precaution against the eventuality of having to leave in a hurry, Joe and Butch had kept the mounts on the outskirts of town on a piece of ground owned by the diner owner.

'Goddamn that interfering, damn-blasted sheriff!' Butch swore. 'Hell! I was just getting to know that gal when that hound dog muscled in. Hell and tarnation, that goddamn sheriff seems hell-bent on stringing me up! And that preacher fella don't sound like he got no Christian forgiving in him.' Butch rubbed his ear, which was still smarting from the bucket wielded by Reverend Dinwiddie. 'I reckon he'll be as hell-bent on stringing me up as that goddamn sheriff.'

'Mister, put your hands in the air, slow and steady. There's two guns

14

aimed at your back right now and we both of us got itchy fingers. Just one wrong move and Reverend Dinwiddie will be preaching a funeral service just for you.'

Butch hesitated, wondering if he could slide beneath his horse and get his gun into play before a bullet slowed him down. The explosion of a gunshot made him jump and something whistled over his head. The saddled horses jerked nervously on their halters.

'Next one's in the back of your head, buster.'

Butch gave in and raised his hands in the air. There was movement behind him and he felt his gun being lifted.

'We knowed you were holding your horses down here, and Sheriff Richards reckoned if you slipped by him, this is where you would head. He's had us staked out here all evening which is not a duty we are partial to. So mister, if you're thinking of causing trouble, I'd as soon put you in the dirt with this here pistol and take you into town tied over that saddle as walk you in.'

'I'll come quiet.'

'Good decision, owlhoot. Put your hands behind your back.'

Butch obeyed and handcuffs clicked around his wrists.

While Butch was being arrested Sheriff Richards had not been idle either. He staggered out of the livery. Blood leaked from his mouth where Butch had kicked him and broken his jaw. For a moment Sheriff Richards looked around wildly, then he spun round and went back inside the livery.

Reverend Dinwiddie was standing before a chastened Josephine and preaching to her as only a preacher and a father can.

'Jezebel brought disgrace on herself and womenfolk, and that's not what I reared my daughter for. You will get down on your knees this minute, young woman, and beg the good Lord's forgiveness. When we get home I'll chastise you with a strip of rawhide across your backside . . . '

'Rebend . . . ' The sheriff's damaged mouth seriously hindered speaking. 'Warn tha cluch ball!'

The preacher stared askance at the lawman.

'What are you doing back here? I thought you would be in pursuit of that reprobate who tried to lead my daughter into the paths of iniquity.'

'Wam tha cuch ball!'

It took some time for Sheriff Richards to make sense of what the preacher required of him. In the end it was Josephine who interpreted for him.

'He wants you to ring the church bell, Father. It's the alarm to rouse the town.'

Josephine immediately regretted her impulse to aid her father and the sheriff. She had only known Butch Shilton for a short time. He had swept her off her feet; he was so different from the local men, who tiptoed around her, fearful of her fire-breathing preacher of a father. Reverend Dinwiddie hurried off to the church.

The tolling of the church bell in the evening was such an unusual event that it did indeed bring people out into the streets. They instinctively headed towards the jailhouse and encountered the sheriff making his way there also. He was being assisted by Josephine and when the crowd gathered she was obliged to act as his spokesperson.

'Sheriff Richards was attacked by someone down at the livery. The man escaped.'

'Bluh Thillon.'

Sheriff Richards wanted the villain identified, but was saved the bother, for at that moment his deputies pushed a handcuffed man into the centre of the crowd.

Josephine stared with some distress at the captive. To see her admirer handcuffed like a felon was breaking her young heart. Sheriff Richards came up close to the prisoner and stared hard at him. He pointed to his broken jaw, then drew back his fist and smashed it into Butch's face. Butch's captors grabbed him before he fell, and dragged him towards the jail.

'I guess he's in for a hard time with Sheriff Richards.'

In spite of the unfortunate start to the evening, the sheriff's plan was coming together as he espied two more of his deputies escorting a big man towards the jail. The crowd parted to let the trio through. Joe Peters, manacled, and under the guns of the two deputies, was marched inside the jail.

'What they done, Sheriff?' someone in the crowd called.

For answer the sheriff pulled out a Wanted notice and held it up. He pointed to the bill, then turned and disappeared inside the jail. Josephine followed him. Knowing it was useless to ask the sheriff, she addressed herself to one of the deputies.

'What's going to happen to those men now?'

Instead of giving her an answer, and keeping his voice low as if he did not want anyone to overhear, the deputy asked a question of Josephine.

'You any idea how the sheriff ended up with a busted jaw?'

'He . . . Mr Shilton attacked him, that's how.'

'It figures. You can see how riled up the sheriff is. He's one unforgiving son-abitch, begging your pardon, ma'am. You saw how he punched that fella out there in front of the jail. My guess is he'll more than likely hang them.'

'He can't just hang them without some sort of authorization. Surely there must be a trial?'

The deputy's mouth turned down.

'Don't count on it, Miss Josephine. Sheriff Richards ain't one to care much about regulations. He's of the old school. Shoot first and ask questions later. The Wanted poster says 'dead or alive'. The sheriff knows he'll collect the reward however he delivers them two owlhoots, dead or alive.'

4

Josephine left the sheriff's office, her mind in turmoil. The deputy's predictions as to the fate of Butch and his partner Joe Peters were too awful for her young mind to contemplate. Despondently she turned towards home, knowing that what awaited her there was the nagging voice of her father preaching at her for her waywardness.

'Miss Josephine.'

She looked up as her name was called. Widow Ellison, the owner of the local diner, was approaching.

'What's all the excitement? I heard the church bell ringing.'

'They caught two men the sheriff claims are on the run,' Josephine answered dully.

'Two men? What two men?'

'Butch Shilton and Joe Peters.'

'Joe Peters? There must be some mistake. That man ain't no outlaw.'

Josephine burst into tears. Maud moved close and put her arms around the young woman.

'There, there, dear, you come on down to my place. What you need is a mug of coffee — or something stronger.'

While they sipped their coffee, liberally laced with bourbon, Josephine told the older woman all that had happened.

'And now he's in jail,' she wailed. 'And it's my fault.'

'Hush now, Josephine, drink up your coffee. It ain't no one's fault. You say as Butch broke the sheriff's jaw?'

Josephine nodded miserably. Now that the whiskey was taking effect her tears were flowing freely. Suddenly Maud began to giggle.

'Sheriff Richards with a broken jaw,' she chortled gleefully. 'Serve the old galoot right.'

'I don't know what's so funny,'

Josephine said tearfully. 'I reckon that's the reason the sheriff is going to hang Butch — to get his own back.'

'No, you're quite right, my dear, it ain't funny. It's just as Sheriff Stanley Richards comes in my diner, orders a meal and more time than enough leaves without paying.'

'Why, that's awful. That's . . . that's like stealing.'

'You're damn right it is. If his jaw is broke, then it'll be a while afore he's fit to eat again. That's why I was laughing. Serves the thieving old galoot right.'

In spite of her distress Josephine smiled through her tears.

'Poetic justice,' she murmured. 'It was the sheriff who brought Pa down the lively to catch Butch and me together. That was mean. He could have left Pa out of it. All he was really after was Butch. It was so humiliating.'

The two women sat silent, sunk in their own thoughts, drinking alcohol-laced coffee.

'There's a way to get back at them, you know,' Maud said thoughtfully after a bit. 'And at the same time help those two poor men in jail.'

'Tell me.'

The alcohol in the coffee was taking effect and Josephine, unused to strong beverages, was feeling light-headed and reckless. So Maud told her what they could do to prevent a miscarriage of justice and get one over on Sheriff Stanley Richards who, by his boorish behaviour, had set the two women so much against him.

★ ★ ★

The jailhouse door rattled loudly. The deputy left in charge of the prisoners looked up in annoyance.

'What in tarnation?' he grumbled as he went to open up.

He blinked in surprise at the sight of the two women laden with trays waiting patiently on the step.

'Supper for the prisoners,' Maud

announced breezily, pushing past the deputy.

Josephine smiled demurely at the bemused man and followed Maud inside.

'I . . . when was this ordered?'

'Oh, it wasn't ordered,' Josephine told him. 'I took it on myself to ask Mrs Ellison if she would assist me in making Sheriff Richards's job a mite easier, taking some of the responsibility off him. Seeing as the sheriff was indisposed I guessed he would have forgotten to feed the prisoners, and I felt it was my Christian duty to feed the poor and needy and distressed.' She giggled. 'Not that you're poor and needy, Deputy Grimbley, but I could not leave you out.'

The deputy's face brightened.

'You brought me supper, Miss Josephine? That is sure mighty Christian of you.'

He moved back to the desk and watched as Josephine put the tray down.

'Shall I take this through to the cells?' Maud asked.

'Sure, sure,' Deputy Grimbley said absently, his eyes fixed on the tray Josephine was uncovering.

'I hope you got a sweet tooth, Deputy. Mrs Ellison included some apple pie and molasses.'

Mrs Ellison disappeared out the back into the cell block with her tray. Joe jumped to his feet as he saw who it was.

'Maud!'

'Joe, I brought you and Butch some supper. You must be right hungry after all you been through.' She bent and slid the tray under the door, 'Take care with the chicken pie. I don't want you to break a tooth.' She smiled sweetly and curtsied. 'Good luck, Joe Peters, and may God go with you.' Then she was gone.

'You think she was a mite tearful?' Joe said wistfully.

Butch did not reply immediately. He was examining the contents of the tray.

'Goddamn, Joe! The condemned

men ate a hearty supper. Chicken pie and potatoes and what looks like apple pie. You ought to marry that Widow Ellison.'

'Yeah, and make her a widow for the fourth time when they take us out to hang us.' Joe frowned suddenly. 'What the hell she mean — don't break a tooth on the chicken pie? Maud's pies are real easy-eating.'

Joe picked up a fork and poked it through the piecrust. The prongs did not go far before hitting something solid. Thoughtfully, Joe peeled back the pastry. Steam rose from the fresh-baked pie. He dug the fork in deeper and encountered something large and unyielding that was no part of a chicken's anatomy.

Gingerly he pushed the fork beneath the object and exposed a well-wrapped shape that had a remarkable resemblance to a gun. Joe looked up at Butch and smiled as he hooked out the bundle.

'Chicken-and-pistol pie. Now ain't

that something.'

He peeled back the waxed paper protecting the gun from the pie-filling.

'Right.' Butch was standing by the door of the cell. 'When you're ready I'll call the guard down.'

Joe carefully checked the weapon. It was a Colt .38, fully loaded and appeared to be in perfect working order. The big man laid the weapon on the bunk behind him.

'Has that punch from Sheriff Richards rattled your brain or something?' Joe spread his hands over the tray of food. 'There's a wholesome supper here awaiting to be ate. I ain't escaping until I store this here chicken pie inside me.'

Butch cast his eyes skywards. Then the smell of the food hit him.

'Hell! Maybe you're right. I wouldn't want you to faint from lack of food afore we hit the trail again.'

5

'Aw, man,' Joe Peters sat back on the jailhouse bunk with a contented sigh. 'Widow Ellison, you're every eating man's dream come true.'

At that moment Sheriff Stanley Richards came to the cell door. The lower part of his face was bandaged. He glared balefully in at the prisoners, then stared at the trayful of empty dishes. He made a pantomime of tying a knot in a rope and settling a pretend noose over his head, hanging his head to one side and making ghastly strangling noises. With a broken and bandaged jaw it was the best he could do. Deputy Grimbley appeared behind the sheriff.

'Sheriff wants you fellas to sleep easy tonight. He reckons it'll be your last night on earth. First light he reckons to take you fellas out and hang you.'

Joe stood up.

'He can't do that. We got rights. We committed no crime in this state. He has to hand us over to the federal authorities.'

Joe walked over to the cell door, his hands outstretched as if pleading for mercy. The smuggled pistol was tucked into his belt in the small of his back, out of sight of the lawmen.

'Push that tray out under the door,' the deputy ordered. 'Sheriff Richards is worried you might make some sort of weapon out of that stuff.'

Butch came forward. Using his foot he pushed the tray towards the front of the cell. Joe was against the bars, pleading with the sheriff.

'Sheriff, I'm sorry about your busted jaw. Can't you show us some pity?'

If his face had been fully exposed the sheriff might have been observed snarling. He stepped closer to the cell door and glared at the big man, hatred in his eyes.

'I guess not,' Joe said regretfully.

Butch reached casually behind Joe,

pulled the .38 from his belt and pushed the barrel into the bandage on the sheriff's face.

'Sheriff, you still got a jaw left that might heal over time. If I pull this trigger there'll be a hole in your head that'll never get a chance to heal. So you tell your man here to unlock this door real careful.'

The two lawmen froze, staring wide-eyed at Butch.

'You know my reputation. I've already killed two lawmen.'

Which wasn't true, but Butch needed every edge he could think of to get out of jail; the more ruthless the lawmen believed him to be the more chance he had of making them obey him.

'Two more notches on my gun don't make no difference to me. So if you fellas want to live beyond tonight, you do as I tell you and unlock this cell door.'

To emphasize his threat Butch thumbed back the hammer on the revolver. The loud click of the mechanism in his face made the sheriff flinch. Afraid to move his bust jaw away from the gun he slowly raised his hand and motioned to his deputy, pointing to the cell door. Butch smiled grimly.

'Now we'll find out if this fella is after your job, Sheriff. If I shoot you, is he next in line?'

'I ain't wanting no such thing,' said the deputy hastily. 'Don't you shoot. I got the key right here.'

After a bit of fumbling the deputy unlocked the door and the two prisoners stepped free.

'Weapons, Joe,' Butch said.

Quickly Joe disarmed the lawmen, pushed them inside the cell and relocked the door.

'You're lucky you caught him in a good mood,' Joe told the two men. 'When I told him about that gun I had hidden in my britches he was all for shooting his way out of here, but luckily I persuaded him otherwise.'

Butch pointed the gun inside the cell.

'You fellas keep quiet till we're clear.

Otherwise I'll likely regret my decision not to kill you.'

The lawmen stared balefully back at him, making no response.

'Come on, Butch. The sooner we're out of here the better.'

The prisoners left the cells and moved into the main office.

'See if you can find our weapons,' said Butch, 'while I have a look out the front to make sure the coast is clear.'

No sooner had Joe started searching than there sounded the most almighty racket coming from the cell block. Sheriff Richards had picked up a tin mug from the supper tray and was hammering on the bars of the cell. Deputy Grimbley was at the barred window, yelling at the top of his voice.

'Help! Help! The prisoners are escaping! Help!'

'Hell damnit, Joe! They'll rouse the whole goddamn town. We should have tied up those two varmints and gagged them. Grab what weapons you can and let's get out of here.'

Joe snatched up a couple of gunbelts and slung one across to Butch. They crashed out through the front door to find that some of the townspeople were coming up the street.

'That's them outlaws!'

Bullets peppered the front of the building where the two escaped men were standing.

'Damnit to hell! Put a few over their heads to slow them down,' Butch yelled. He fired towards the oncoming men.

The shots were enough to scatter the townsfolk and the escapers turned and ran along the boardwalk.

'Make for the horses,' Butch panted. 'I saddled up afore they took me prisoner. Hopefully the horses are still down there. If not, we'll have a helluva job fighting our way out of this hellhole of a town.'

Behind them there was some yelling and shots came their way. The fugitives turned a corner; for a while they were out of sight of the pursuing towns-people.

'Hell damnit! I wish I hadn't had extra helpings of that apple pie,' Joe puffed. 'It's slowing me down some.'

'I always said your eating would get you in trouble some day.'

'I heard a fella claim once,' Joe panted, 'that you dig your own grave with your teeth. I never did understand that till right now.'

'Keep going, Joe. We're nearly there.'

Butch was running easily, keeping pace with his companion and glancing from time to time over his shoulder. The section came in sight and the horses could be seen waiting patiently, still saddled and tied up where Butch had left them.

'Thank God for that!'

But even as they mounted up shots came whistling their way. Frantically heeling the horses into action they rode out into the night. Soon they were out of gunshot range but they kept up their furious pace. They were both aware that Sheriff Richards would not rest up, injured jaw or not. The vindictive lawman would most likely organize a chase. For the moment Butch and Joe had a head start, but soon there would be a posse hot on their heels.

6

Dusty and travel-stained, the wanted men sat their mounts and gazed at the signpost.

'Barbelle, three miles,' Joe read. 'What do you think, Butch, should we chance it?'

'Barbelle. I like the sound of that, Joe. It conjures up images of saloons and cathouses and frolicking females.'

'Frolicking females?' The big man shook his head in exasperation. 'That's what got us in trouble the last place we were at. You had to go sparking the minister's daughter. For Gawd's sake, the Reverend Dinwiddie's daughter! I had to pull your ass out of the fire *once again* when you got yourself arrested.'

'What the hell do you mean? Don't forget you were in jail along with me. I'd have got out of jail without your help.'

'Oh yeah? I was in jail because I planned it that way.'

'You planned it? How can you plan to have yourself arrested?'

'Listen, you dog-brained jackass, any fool can get himself arrested. The real test is getting back out of jail. I had it all figured. I got myself arrested after arranging for Maud to smuggle me a gun. That's what's called strategy. Whereas you — you go and bust the sheriff's jaw. That's what got him so riled up as he was going to hang us.'

'Hell! A fella's got a right to defend himself.'

'There's defending yourself and there's breaking the law. And then there's breaking the lawman's jaw when he came to arrest you.'

'It was self-defence. He was about to put a slug in me. I had to disarm him somehow even if it did mean breaking his goddamn jaw.'

'Yeah, and fancy taking Josephine, the preacher's daughter into the livery stable. Any fool could have told you that was asking for trouble.'

'Josephine.' A dreamy look came over Butch's face. 'She was exquisite, the body of Aphrodite and the mind of Joan of Arc'

Joe was looking at his companion with a perplexed frown on his face.

'What the hell's Joan of Arc got to do with the Reverend Dinwiddie's daughter?'

'Joan was touched by God, as was the divine Josephine.'

'She was touched all right, touched in the head to get involved with a lowlife like you.'

'You take that back, Joe Peters. I ain't no lowlife.'

'Look at you.' Joe laughed scornfully. 'You're a saddle bum — a wanted man.'

'I ain't no saddle bum, no matter what the hell you say. And anyway it's the tub calling the kettle black.'

'You got that wrong. It's the pot and the kettle, the pot calling the kettle black.'

'I know what I'm saying. When I say

tub, I mean tub, a tub of lard is what I mean.'

'Take that back, you son of a bitch! I can tell you this is all muscle.' Joe sat up straight in the saddle and sucked in his stomach as he spoke.

'Huh!'

The partners glared at each other for moments, wondering if it was worth getting down off their horses and settling the disagreement with a bout of fisticuffs.

'Hell, Joe! I owe you one for busting me out of that jail, but you never arranged nothing. It was Maud as felt sorry for you and decided to help us. We sure owe that female our lives.' Butch swivelled around in the saddle. 'I just hope we lost that posse back there.'

The fugitives glanced uneasily over their shoulders.

'Come on. I'm tired of running. Let's go down to this here Barbelle and have us a beer and a steak and then light out again for the border. I reckon we lost that posse long back.'

Barbelle, so near the Mexican border, was a town with a mixed population of Mexicans and Americans. No one took any notice of the newcomers. Butch and Joe chose a cantina full to bursting with a noisy mix of *vaqueros* and American cowboys.

Consciously avoiding the Americans, the newcomers squeezed in with a crowd of boisterous Mexicans who had bottles of rum and tequila on the table. Women were busy ferrying food from the kitchen. While Butch and Joe waited to be served, the Mexicans welcomed the newcomers and invited them to share a drink with them.

'You have come far, *amigos*?' one man asked, eyeing the dusty condition of their garments. 'You must be thirsty.'

'Thirsty, *sí*, I'm dry as a widow's ass.'

When this piece of wisdom had been relayed to the table there was much merriment amongst the drinkers. Upon realizing that their new companions were hungry as well as thirsty the Mexicans hollered and banged the table for the attention of the serving women. They then took over the ordering, starting the strangers off with eggs and chilli peppers

'Goddamn it, these peppers are hotter than Beelzebub's armpits,' Butch gasped, his eyes watering as he chewed. 'My stomach feels like it's being scrubbed down with a yard brush dipped in lye.'

The Mexicans roared with laughter and encouraged him to wash down the fiery mix with tequila. Joe was shovelling in huge mouthfuls and showing every sign of enjoying the hot fare.

Steaks and tortillas came next, followed by platters of *frijoles* all washed down with more tequila. Butch threw in the towel after the first platter of *frijoles* but Joe was not finished yet, not by a long chalk. If there was one thing Joe was good at, it was eating. More steak and tortillas were brought out. The Mexicans watched in awe as Joe cleared his plate, then raised his

42

eyebrows and held out his hands, palms up.

'Is that it?'

Their hosts roared with delight, hammered on the table and ordered another plate of eggs and peppers. Joe was in good eating form; chilli peppers along with the eggs disappeared rapidly as the big man washed them down with large draughts of tequila.

'Bravo! Bravo!' the Mexicans yelled as the eggs disappeared down Joe's gullet. They banged the table and ordered more eggs and tequila.

'Hey, you slimy greasers, keep that bastard noise down.' The speaker was a big man in a buckskin jacket; his skin also had the appearance of cured leather. He was at the next table with a group of equally tough-looking companions. They carried large knives in leather scabbards along with holstered pistols.

The Mexicans became quiet and looked with some hostility at the Americans. For some moments the

Americans glared back, the tension building. Joe Peters swallowed an egg and wiped his hand on his shirt.

'Did I just hear someone fart out of his face?' he said loudly. He turned and glared at the bearded man who had objected to the noise from Joe's table. 'Mister, you smell like a buffalo's asshole.'

'Joe,' Butch pleaded, 'not now, not here. We've only come in for a quick drink and a bite to eat.'

Butch might as well not have spoken for all the notice Joe took of him. Large quantities of tequila have the effect of blunting a man's good sense.

'In fact, now that I got a good look at you,' Joe blundered on, 'your face bears a remarkable resemblance to a buffalo's rear end. Assholes shouldn't be eating in the same room as normal folk. You fellas take this bottom-feeder outside so as he don't stink up the place where decent folk are eating and drinking.'

'Goddamn!' roared the bearded man.

44

'I don't take that from no man.'

He was struggling to his feet when Joe hurled the empty *frijoles* bowl at him, splitting the skin on his temple.

'Waagh . . . '

For a big man, when Joe wanted to move fast he was as quick as any man half his size. He took everyone by surprise and was on his feet as the man he had hit with the platter was still trying to disentangle his limbs from his table. Joe smashed his fist into the cowboy's face.

'Oh no,' Butch groaned. He grabbed up a chair and broke it over the head of one of the Americans as he too struggled to his feet to come to the aid of his companion.

'Yeehaar!'

Joe threw himself forward and took two more of the bearded Americans to the floor. Butch retained a portion of the broken chair and smashed it into the hand of one of men coming off the bench with his knife out.

'Damn you, Joe Peters!' Butch

45

grunted as yet another two big bearded men came at him. 'A steak and a beer and then we were supposed to be out of here.'

Now he was fighting on two fronts, kicking and punching as he was attacked. Beside him Joe rose up like a mountain bear, his arms trapping the heads of the two men he had wrestled to the floor. The heads crashed together as Joe flexed his arms. The struggling Americans went limp.

The remaining three Americans were coming to their feet to rescue their companions. One was drawing his pistol. Joe grabbed hold of the table, which was fashioned from thick, rough-hewn boards, and picked it up as if it were no heavier than a flimsy chair. With a bearlike roar he lunged at the Americans, knocking them to the floor. Joe yelled again with joy of battle and flung himself on top of the upended table. The downed men stood no chance as the heavy table, with the powerful frame of Joe Peters weighing it down, crushed them into screaming submission.

Gunshots blasted into the air. The fighters paused, gradually becoming aware that men with drawn guns were surrounding them. Ominously, as far as Joe and Butch were concerned, not only were these men pointing guns: all were sporting badges. One of the lawmen stepped forward and picked out Joe and Butch.

'Well, well, well, what have we got here? I got a wire from Sheriff Richards saying you two hellions might be heading this way. He told me to hang you, but I got a better idea. You're headed for a long spell in the penitentiary, where you will have plenty of leisure time to repent your evil ways.'

The lawmen backing him up tittered as if sharing some private joke.

7

The prisoners stood in line in a courtyard beneath a burning sun. They were in a square in which adobe buildings were enclosed within a high wall. Towers at each corner housed guards with rifles who were idly keeping watch on the prisoners within the courtyard. This was Los Pecos penitentiary.

There came the sound of iron striking iron as the new prisoners were fitted with manacles.

'Next.'

Propelled by a violent shove Joe stumbled forward and obediently placed his right foot on the anvil. The blacksmith clamped the iron ring on his ankle, hammered in a crude rivet to secure it and waited for the left foot to be presented. The process was efficient and in a short time each newcomer was fitted with leg irons connected by a chain. A man so fitted out could not run very fast, nor could he fork a horse. On uneven terrain the chain was inclined to snag on protruding rocks and roots. As well as slowing a man down the shackles were a constant reminder of his slavelike status in his new existence.

Once the blacksmith had finished his work a human snake formed up inside the prison to the sounds of clinking chains, the curses of the guards and the occasional crack of leather against flesh.

'Hell, Joe!' Butch murmured, *sotto voce*, 'we've been here a month and we're no nearer finding a way out of this hell-hole.'

He was taking a risk in speaking even this low, for it was a flogging offence to talk while on a working line. In the time during which they had endured the harsh regime, Butch had received several floggings for some misdemeanour, real or trumped up. The head warder, Mike Shannon, had taken a particular dislike to Butch and had singled him out for special treatment. Butch's back was raw from the constant whipping.

Right now the convicts were being assembled to march in a chain gang to the silver mine for another exhausting shift. Picks and shovels were stored at the mine and the convicts laboured in the depths of the mountain, hacking at rock walls that bore the marks of tools wielded by previous generations of miners. So deep were they inside the mountain that the atmosphere was oven-hot and breathing was difficult for lack of air.

'Jeez, Butch, I been racking my brain for some scheme to help us break out, but they keep us bottled up so tight it would take a miracle to bust out of this place. Anyway, you're the fella with all the ideas . . . ouch!'

Joe winched as the whip curled out and caught him on the shoulder. Again and again the whip lashed out with unerring accuracy, striking the big man all over his back and shoulders. Chained in the line, it was impossible to escape that hornet sting. Joe cursed silently and raged at his helplessness. Often he imagined getting Shannon on his own, without his whips and his brutal hellions.

'Hold it! Peters and Shilton fall out.'

The two men looked at each other. They knew what was coming. For the last week Shannon had singled out the two men for latrine duty. It was a job that was usually shared out amongst the convicts and was particularly hard work: stinking, brutal, exhausting and soul-destroying.

After cleaning out the jakes the prisoners were then escorted back to the mine to join their comrades for a further shift of exhausting toil. Any convict would gladly have marched to the mines for an extra shift, rather than be assigned to this foul duty.

'Isaac,' Shannon called 'Your turn for latrine duty.'

Isaac Devlin and his brother Jubal

51

were the most sadistic of the prison
guards and meted out punishment at
every opportunity whether it was
earned or not. Isaac, the younger of the
brothers, scowled at his boss.

'Hell, Shannon, can't someone else
take these lunk-heads to the jacks.
That's twice this week I done it.'

'Just do what you're told, Devlin,' the
chief warder snarled, 'and be quick
about it. I want those two dummies
over at the mine *pronto* when they
finished, afore they think they're being
giving special treatment and can slack
off.' He sniggered. 'Make them do the
job double-quick. I want them crawling
over to that mine on their hands and
knees begging to be allowed to pick up
their shovels an' git to work.'

'Yeah, yeah, I hear you.'

Isaac aimed a kick at Butch that
caught him on the back of the leg.
Butch stumbled and almost went down.

'Come on, you goddamn lazy bastards. Git moving,' Isaac growled.

Then he smashed the weighted

handle of the whip on the side of Joe's head. It was a brutal blow, splitting the skin and blood oozed from the wound. Joe jerked away from the guard, put his hand up to his head, then stared at the blood smeared on his hand. With a growl he turned and crashed into Butch who, seeing his pal about to explode, pushed in between the two men.

'Joe, Joe,' Butch said urgently, 'we got work to do.'

An agonizing streak of fire opened new weals on his back as Isaac lashed out in frenzy.

'No talking, you goddamn piece of shit! You want another twenty lashes?'

Yelling abuse, Isaac kept lashing Butch. The two convicts lurched towards the latrine, trying without success to keep out of range of that deadly lash.

Latrine duty was a special type of misery within the hell of Los Pecos prison. Large wooden buckets that held at least a couple of gallons were used to transport the waste matter. Each prisoner assigned to the task was provided with two of these and a wooden shovel. The buckets were filled and then carried to a gully well away from the prison walls.

While the prisoners worked, Isaac stood back from the trench, well out of range of the smell, shouting abuse at the two men.

'Shift your lazy asses, or I'll skin you alive, you pair of deadbeats.'

The prisoners tried to take shallow breaths as they worked. It was all they could do to hold down the cornmeal breakfast they had consumed but a brief time ago.

'Jeez, Joe, another day like this and I'm going to strangle myself with my chain,' gasped Butch.

'Why'd you stop me from throttling that goddamn Isaac back there?' Joe replied as he picked up the shovel and began jabbing it into the trench.

'Hell Joe! You know why. We seen one fella flogged to death for the very same thing.'

'Yeah, well, it's one way of getting out of here.'

'A goddamn painful way. I can still hear that Judd fella screaming as the Brothers Grimm set upon him. What got to me most was the way they were laughing as they set to with those goddamn whips.'

It was painfully slow work. Isaac yelled abuse for a while but even he got tired of the game, while the hot sun beamed down as it did every day.

When the buckets were full they were slung on a thick pole and the whole contraption then had to be balanced across the shoulders and carried. Such was the weight, a man could only shuffle, one step at a time, until he got to the delivery point.

Isaac Devlin stalked behind them and abused them verbally and physically.

'Come on, you lazy sons of bitches, move your asses!'

And the whip would sting whatever part of the anatomy the guard thought would be most painful.

The disposal gully was several hundred yards from the penal complex. When the wind was right, the smell from the waste drifted into the enclosure and made a miserable existence unbearable.

The buckets were lowered to the ground and unhooked from the pole. While trying not to breathe Joe picked up one of the wooden buckets preparatory to adding the contents to the stinking lagoon. That was when Isaac thought to play a prank on the big man.

Stepping up behind his unsuspecting victim, Isaac placed his boot on Joe's rear end and shoved. Joe yelled, dropped the bucket and flailed his arms to stay upright but the laws of gravity kicked in along with the propulsion from Isaac's boot and the big man toppled into the steaming cesspool.

8

Butch heard the yell and looked up just in time to see his comrade topple into the abyss. He looked on in horror as Joe splashed into the stinking ordure.

Butch might have thought Joe had slipped and fallen, but he guessed something more serious had happened. The guard was bent over holding himself as he howled with laughter.

With an effort fuelled by desperation Joe managed to stand upright. Butch could only watch helplessly as his partner wallowed in the muck. Slowly, Joe, like some swamp-beast, waded to the side, reached out and began to haul himself up. The walls of the gully were slimy from old spills and he was finding it difficult to get a purchase.

Seeing his pal's difficulty Butch looked round for some way of helping. He spotted Joe's discarded pole. He ran forward, grabbed it and made to lower it down to the climbing man. He almost yelled out as the familiar pain, like a knife slicing into his back, caused him to leap back.

'What the hell you doing?' snarled Isaac, flicking the whip ready for another strike. 'Who gave you permission to move?'

Butch could only stare resentfully at the guard as he listened to the grunts of his pal struggling to climb from the pit. Out Joe came, groaning with the effort as he heaved himself up and over the edge. Butch watched helplessly as the guard readied the whip. Isaac hesitated, suddenly realizing that to lash Joe, covered in filth as he was, would contaminate the leather.

Like a dog coming to shore out of a river, Joe shook his head to rid himself of the worst of the muck. Breathing heavily the big man raised himself upright. Isaac started laughing again.

'You sure the shittiest booger I ever did see, Peters,' he yelled between bouts of mirth. 'Joe Peters — turdman of Los Pecos.'

Joe stood still for a moment, his arms held out from his body, looking indeed every inch the nickname he'd been given. He looked around him. His gaze rested on the remaining bucket waiting to be emptied into the gully.

'I guess I'd better empty that last bucket,' he said.

Butch felt his guts tighten as he heard that calm statement. He could only look on as he waited for the inevitable. Joe picked up the bucket. Isaac was grinning as he watched.

'Hurry up, shithead, we ain't got all morning to hang around here,' he snarled. 'Shithead!' he suddenly repeated and held his stomach as he chortled gleefully.

'No,' Butch whispered, afraid to speak out loud.

In a few swift strides Joe reached the guard. The bucket swung up and over, as if it were no lighter than a milk pail. Before Isaac could react the bucket was wedged over his head while Joe kneed the guard in the groin. With his head buried inside the bucket Isaac made no sound as he went down.

Keeping a hold on the bucket, Joe went down with him. He ended up sitting on top of Isaac. The whip fell to the ground as the guard grabbed the suffocating thing on his head and tried to force it away.

Looking like some obscene carving in the shape of a man, Joe sat immobile on the guard's chest. Isaac's heels were gouging up divots. The bucket had been full; very little had spilled when it descended on the guard's head. Inside the bucket the filth covered his eyes and ears and nostrils and oozed into his mouth as he opened it to gulp for air.

'Joe, I think he's had enough.' Butch was watching with some concern the consequences of his friend's actions. 'I don't think he'll be able to breathe with that bucket on his head.'

'Push me in the gully!' Joe roared.

'Call me shithead! Who's a shithead now?'

The guard's efforts to free himself were weakening. His hands pawed feebly at Joe's arms as the big man held the wooden bucket in position. Isaac might as well have been trying to root up a tree.

Butch hesitated to grab Joe and force him from his position on top of the squirming guard, for the big man was covered in ordure and Butch was suddenly squeamish about touching him.

'Joe, please . . . '

And then Butch trailed off, realizing that no matter what happened now, they were dead men. Attacking a guard was punishable by a flogging. It would be no ordinary flogging. Joe had just sentenced them both to a horrifically painful death.

The boot heels stopped ploughing their little furrows, the legs relaxed and became still. Hands that had scrabbled at Joe's solid forearms dropped limply to the dirt. Joe sat back on the unmoving guard.

'You think he's dead?'

'If he ain't, he's sure making a pretty good imitation of how a dead man should act. He really push you in?'

'Just as I was swinging the bucket he planted one on me. There was nothing I could do.' Joe shook his head in bewilderment. 'Sure beats me how a man can be so ornery.' Slowly he raised himself from the body and got to his feet. 'Hell Butch, you know what'll happen to us now. They'll hang us for sure.'

'If only that were true, Joe. Hanging would be a blessing compared with what they going to do to us when they find Isaac Devlin dead.'

Joe was holding his hands out from his sides, looking down at the foul mess dripping from his clothes. Butch moved over to the body of the guard and went through the pockets. He removed the gunbelt with the Colt and the scabbard with the Bowie. He also found tobacco and matches along with some loose change. He buckled on the gunbelt and tossed the knife to Joe.

'Cut his pants into strips. We'll use them to tie up these here chains. Make it easier to walk.'

Joe looked at Butch and frowned.

'As soon as I knew you were going to finish that guard I began to figure out our chances,' Butch said. 'So get to work.' He watched as Joe hacked slices from the guard's britches. 'When you finished with him we'll toss him in the gully. I reckon Isaac won't be missed till late afternoon at least, or maybe not until the work shift returns.

'They'll start the search here, because that's where they know we were working. Then they'll figure we went that way.' Butch turned and pointed in a direction parallel with the gully. 'But instead we head for the mine. If we're lucky we'll escape detection, find tools to break these manacles and maybe steal a couple of horses. I know there's a lot of maybes in that, but if we just start running as we are, they'll track us down afore we get very far.'

9

The would-be escapers peered down on the mining development, trying to figure out the best way of getting in without being discovered.

The silver mine was surrounded by a number of ramshackle buildings spread over a couple of acres. An air of neglect hung over everything. Large heaps of mined rocks dotted the area. The buildings were coated in dust that came up from the mine as the ore was extracted from deep inside the mountain.

The dilapidated buildings were used for a variety of functions; some holding old machinery, others serving as bunkhouses and eating quarters for the overseers and engineers who operated the mine.

'We take it easy going in, keeping to cover where we can. The important thing is to find some horses to carry us out of this place. We need something to break these goddamn chains.'

With the strips cut from Isaac's clothing they had made slings to keep the chains from dragging on the ground, but now they needed to rid themselves of the manacles if they proposed to find horses to aid them in escaping beyond the reach of the prison authorities.

There seemed little going on in and around the buildings. Most of the activity was near the main entrance to the mine, where mules dragged buggies of ore to the surface; these were then emptied beside the crusher. Convicts were working at the crusher, loading the mined rock on to the conveyor belt that fed the voracious monster. The noise from the crusher sounded like muted thunder and the nearer to the machine a man stood the more deafening the din became.

While they scanned their surroundings and planned their route through the compound Butch became aware of the stink from his partner. He wrinkled his nose and glanced at the big man crouched beside him.

'Jeez Joe! You smell worse than a buffalo carcass that's been laid out in the prairie for a month.'

'What the hell do you expect, dumb brain?' Joe snarled. 'Maybe I pushed the bucket over the wrong fella. Maybe I should have plastered it over your bald skull. Might have fertilized some hair to grow.'

'Sometimes Joe Peters . . . ' Butch breathed deeply then turned away as the stench from Joe hit him more powerfully. 'Only I don't want to sully myself, I'd punch you back down that hill.'

'You punch me? What would you like on your tombstone, knucklehead?'

The two pals glared at each other, then Butch sighed.

'Hell Joe, let's just get out of this damn mess and then we can row all we want. Just try and keep downwind of me.'

Butch slipped from their hiding-place. Joe glared after him but held his peace as he followed. They came to the wooden shacks that housed the permanent mining staff. As they went further in amongst the buildings, the shacks gave place to stone-built structures, where tools and machinery were stored.

'There must be workshops to repair the equipment used in the mine,' Butch stated. 'There should be axes and hammers and chisels somewhere.'

Joe put out a hand. 'Wait.' He was sniffing the air. 'If I'm not mistaken that's charcoal burning. That's got to be a smithy.'

In a building constructed from rough blocks blasted out of the mine workings, they found what they were searching for. They could even hear the clang of metal on metal. The large wooden doors were open and they peered inside.

A burly man was standing by an anvil wielding a hammer on a heated metal bar. The blacksmith had his back to them and was engrossed in his work. The fugitives slipped inside the forge.

Butch pulled the Colt he had taken from the dead Isaac and stepped forward until he came within the view of the blacksmith. The man looked sideways at Butch but carried on working, hammering rhythmically on the bar as he worked.

'Yeah, what you want?'

'Want some work doing,' Butch answered. He shuffled closer and pulled on the rag that held the chain up off the ground. 'Got some chains as need busting.'

The blacksmith shook his head as he took the bar and plunged it into a tin bath filled with water.

'Can't help you.' He held up the bar he'd been working on, critically examined it, then thrust it into the brazier and pumped the bellows. The flames roared in the furnace and glowed with a white-hot intensity.

'You don't understand, mister. This is a Colt .45. When I pull this little trigger here, it goes off and propels a small lead bullet that will blow your tiny little brain out of that thick skull of yours.'

The man suddenly started sniffing.

'What the hell's that goddamn smell?'

'That's my friend standing behind you. He fell in a cesspit and he's mighty mad about it. So don't rile him none and just do as you're told and then you might just survive to shoe another few horses.'

The blacksmith was twisting tire iron bar in the fire.

'Is that so?' As he spoke he pulled the bar from the fire and tossed it at Butch while at the same time swinging around, his hammer raised. Joe's hand closed on the man's wrist and stopped him in mid-arc. At the same time he punched hard into the man's abdomen.

'Goddamn!' the blacksmith roared as he was driven back against the furnace. Even as Joe kneed him in the groin the big man leapt forward from the red-hot forge. He bent forward, gasping in pain.

Joe, using his fist like a hammer, brought it down hard on the back of the man's head. The blacksmith went down and stayed down.

'Why the goddamn hell does everybody have to be so damn ornery!' Joe yelled. 'All we wanted was a little cooperation.'

The injured man made no answer but rolled around on the dirt floor, moaning. Joe looked over at Butch.

'You OK?'

'Sure. I had to dodge that hot iron he threw at me. Hell, I nearly pulled the trigger of this here gun. Let's get some rope and tie up the crazy booger.'

Joe was looking speculatively at the blacksmith.

'Mister, I want you shuck them there duds you're wearing. I need a change of clothing.'

'Go to hell!'

Joe raised his eyes heavenwards.

'Nothing's ever easy in this life, is it?'

10

'Butch, hold up there. Do you see what I see?'

The fugitives were threading their way through the maze of ramshackle buildings that surrounded the mouth of the mineshaft, when Joe hauled up and pointed to a single-storey stone building.

The big man had burned the soiled prison clothing in the furnace when he'd changed into the blacksmith's garments. Joe had also scrubbed his hair and face in the water the blacksmith had been using for cooling off the metal bars. He was now more like his normal self. Butch looked where Joe was pointing. He frowned at the crude sign painted on the large wooden doors.

'No Smoking,' he read. 'Dynamite.' Then he shrugged. 'So what? Neither of us smokes, and shortly we'll be well away from here.'

'Don't you see? Dynamite and stuff that might be useful if the prison guards come in hot pursuit.' Joe moved over to the stout wooden doors. They were secured by a sturdy padlock. 'Wait here, Butch. I'll go back and fetch something from the forge to break this lock.'

'Well, hurry. The longer we stay in this goddamn place the more chance we'll be discovered.'

Joe returned with the hammer and chisel that they had used to break their manacles. A couple of sharp blows and the lock dropped to the dirt.

'Keep watch. I'll grab what I can.'

Joe disappeared inside the building, leaving Butch to pace nervously up and down outside.

'Goddamn it, Joe! Hurry it up,' he muttered. 'An' don't blow yourself up in there.'

The minutes dragged by. It seemed to Butch his companion had been gone for far too long. He became more and more impatient.

'For gawd's sake, Joe! What the hell's keeping you?'

He stuck his head inside the door and then he had a shock. Joe was holding a lighted match as he pulled candle-like objects from a broken box and dropped them into a gunnysack.

'Joe!' Butch squeaked. 'No matches.'

At that point Joe swore and dropped the match as it burned his fingers. Butch hesitated in the doorway, not sure whether to run or stay and die in the explosion he was sure was about to erupt. But no such cataclysm happened and Joe strolled out, carrying the bulging gunnysack.

'Hold this,' he said, pushing the sack at Butch.

Butch backed away.

'That's dynamite in there,' he yelped. 'You had a lighted match.'

'For gawd's sake, Butch! It needs a fuse to set it off. And anyway it was dark in there.'

Joe placed the sack on the ground,

pulled the doors to and fixed the padlock so that it looked as if it were still secure.

'Come on,' Butch said impatiently, 'we got to find us some horses.'

Searching through the maze of buildings, they eventually found the livery. The horses in the stables were workhorses used for hauling the heavy ore wagons to the nearest railhead. There were also saddles and bridles in a bad state of neglect.

'Don't look like they ride much around here.' As the two men saddled the nags they kept expecting the alarm to go up. But all remained quiet at the mine compound, and eventually, sweating and edgy, they were ready.

'Let's walk them a bit,' Butch suggested.

Once they were well away from the mining compound they felt safe enough to climb aboard their new mounts.

They rode steadily for the rest of the day. Butch was eyeing the sky and angling their course ever more southerly. They were threading through a maze of ravines, sometimes coming to a dead end and having to retrace their steps again, but mostly making good progress.

'Travelling over this rock will make it hard to track us. If all goes well they won't discover we're missing till the end of the work shift. Once we get over the border we'll be out of their jurisdiction. With a bit of luck we'll never set eyes on the poisonous brood from Los Pecos ever again.'

'Whoopee!' Joe suddenly yelled. 'We did it. Joe Peters and Butch Shilton jumped ship and have gone missing. Free! We're free!'

The two pals grinned at each other.

'No more latrine duty.'

'No more hacking at that goddamn rock inside that mine.'

'No more floggings.'

'No more of that stinking mess they feed us on. Which reminds me — we ain't got no food, Butch. Ain't much point escaping prison in order to starve to death in these here hills.'

'Joe, what the hell's the matter with you? We escape from a living death and you start moaning about your empty belly. In all your life have you ever gone without?'

'Well no, but that ain't no matter. I'm talking about the here and now. If we don't get food and water soon . . . ' Joe trailed off as if he were not able to contemplate the dire consequences of wandering the passes and ravines without sustenance.

'You know, I been thinking. That was one of the Devlin boys you disposed of back there. His brother Jubal will come after us. According to the other prisoners, there's a whole family of Devlins, all as evil as each other. Some of them work at the mine.'

Joe was nodding thoughtfully. 'The head warden, Shannon, was uncle to that poisonous pair. I guess there's a possibility they'll gather the clan and come after us, right enough.'

'If that's the case, then even if we do cross over the border into Mexico that ain't going to stop them coming after us.'

'Oh, they'll come after us all right. By the way, don't look up, but not far ahead someone has a rifle on us.'

A bearded man was standing on the trail. He was wearing a sombrero along with a full bandoleer crossed on his chest. The rifle he was holding was pointing directly at the two travellers.

'Welcome, *señores*, you look to be lost. Perhaps I can help. Of course there will be a price to pay for my assistance: your money, your horses and maybe your lives. The last depends on how much money you can pay.'

Then more armed men appeared, also with bandoleers across their chests and also carrying weapons.

'*Banditos*,' Butch said, keeping his eye on the armed men.

'*Sí, señor*,' the bearded man agreed.

11

The trail Butch and Joe had been following gradually tapered down to a rocky ravine with boulders littering the sides. The narrowness of the trail had made an ideal ambush site for the bandits, but the hefty boulders at the side of the trail also provided cover for the men they had waylaid.

'I guess it's time for a smoke.'

Joe pulled a small cigarillo from his pocket and struck a match to light it. Butch looked with some surprise at his partner.

'Smoke? Since when did you start smoking?'

'Just this minute,' Joe answered. 'Found these smokes in that blacksmith's pockets. Filthy habit, but when a man's about to die he can take a liking for the most pernicious of habits,'

'Come, *señor*,' the bandit was getting

impatient. 'Throw down your guns and then your money in that order.'

'Pull your revolver, Butch and hold it up so as the fella in the sombrero can see it, then tell him it's all the weapons we got.' Joe gave Butch sight of a piece of fuse fizzing away, but hidden from the bandits by the pummel of his saddle. 'When I throw this, jump for the side of the trail.'

'*Sí*,' Butch answered and held the Colt up in the air.

With a swift movement Joe threw the stick of dynamite while at the same time rolling from the top of his mount. Just in time Butch also vacated his saddle as the bandits opened fire, bullets cutting the space where he had been sitting but a heartbeat before.

The bandits were so busy shooting at the two men diving for cover that they missed the significance of the object sailing through the air towards them. The dynamite hit the side of the ravine and bounced back on to the trail.

As their quarry went to earth some of

the bandits glanced curiously down at the smoking tube that had come to rest a few feet from them. Recognizing it now for what it was they yelled out a warning, then turned to run.

Joe had grabbed the sack of dynamite as he dismounted and taken it with him. He was well hidden behind a large rock when the first stick went off. The detonation in the confined space was deafening. Pieces of rock and debris rained down on him. By now Joe had another stick ready. Someone was screaming but no more shots were coming their way.

'Keep your head down while I chuck another,' he yelled at Butch.

There was no response and Joe glared across the short space that separated him from his partner.

'Oh, no!'

Butch was slumped behind a large boulder, taking no interest in the action.

'Damnit!'

Joe lit a second stick of dynamite

and, without risking raising his head to look at his target, flung it with all his force towards the bandits' position. When the explosion came he leapt across the short distance and crouched beside Butch. The screaming ceased with the second explosion.

'Butch? Goddamn it, Butch! What the hell's the matter with you?'

Then he spotted a swelling as big as a hen's egg on the side of Butch's head; from it a trickle of blood was seeping.

'Butch, this is one helluva time to be taking a nap on me.'

Joe retrieved the pistol that Butch still gripped in his hand and cautiously peered around the side of the boulder. He blinked. Dust was settling in the still, hot air and there was no one standing on the trail. From his restricted view he could see bodies scattered around where the explosions had taken place.

'Hell! Did I do that?'

Slowly he stood up, Colt at the ready. He paced forward.

'*Madre de Dios*, help me ... ' someone was moaning, over and over again.

Joe thrust the Colt under his belt and went back to where he had left Butch. To his relief his partner groaned and opened his eyes. When he recognized Joe he looked at him with a dazed expression.

'Joe ... wha ... what the hell happened?'

Gingerly Butch fingered the lump on his head. 'Goddamn head hurts like the blazes.'

'Reckon you were felled by a piece of rock. Must have been flung up by the explosion. You were lucky it was your head as was hit.'

Butch looked up at the big man, frowning.

'What the hell you mean by that?'

'Aw, you'll figure it out in time.'

'What about those Mex bandits?'

'I don't think we'll have any more bother with them. The explosion kind of knocked them over. I chucked two sticks of explosives but I think one would have been enough.'

'Joe, one thing I can't figure was how the hell you got that dynamite rigged so fast.'

'Well, that was the reason as I took so long at the dynamite shed. I was getting a few ready just in case we needed them to help us escape from the Los Pecos mine.'

By now Butch had got himself on to his feet. His face was pale and he was standing unsteadily.

'Take it easy, Butch,' cautioned Joe. 'That was a nasty crack on the head you got. I'll go see if I can help any of these injured Mexicans.'

'I'll be OK. What happened to our horses?'

Joe glanced around. 'Hell, they must have bolted when the explosions went off. Anyway, maybe we can borrow a couple of mounts from those bandits. Some of them won't be needing them no more, sure as shootin'.'

They found one of the bandits still

alive. He swore feebly at them as Joe cushioned his head and tried to make him comfortable.

'You are dead men,' the Mexican managed to utter.

Butch glanced around at the bloody remains of the man's companions. 'I think you are mistaken, friend. It is your comrades who are dead men. Though I will admit I got one hell of a headache.'

'Barca is not one to take lightly the killing of his men. He will come after you and you will die slowly, maybe two, three days.'

'Who the hell is Barca? Never heard of him.'

But the wounded Mexican started to cough and blood flowed over his lips and ran down his chin. His head lolled to one side as he died.

'Butch, we better hightail it out of here afore this Barca fella comes along and decides to take revenge on us for wiping out his gang of cut-throats.'

They stripped the bodies of guns and

ammunition. By the time they had finished they had gathered a considerable armoury. They donned gunbelts and took a selection of knives for each of them, along with carbines.

'We should try and find these Mexes' horses, seeing as ours seem to have vamoosed,' suggested Joe.

The pair of them set off along the trail.

12

Butch and Joe found the horses further up the trail where it widened considerably. The animals had been hobbled and a rope slung to keep them corralled in one place. In the saddle-bags they found cornbread, jerky and several bottles of tequila. After the weeks of prison fare it was a feast for the two hungry fugitives.

'Man, I never tasted anything so good,' Joe remarked as he washed down the meal with a slug of tequila. He wiped his lips with the back of his hand and stood regarding the horses that they had suddenly acquired. 'What are we going to do with all these here horses?'

'I've been thinking about that. We got seven good pieces of horseflesh here. We take them with us and do a bit of bartering with them. Get us a stake to buy supplies and then we can travel on down to Mexico and get lost so as Jubal Devlin don't find us.'

'I don't like it,' Joe said. 'What about this Barca fella? If he catches up with us and we have all those horses as belonged to his gang then he'll know for sure we must have finished them off. They'll hang us, ain't no doubtin'.'

'Barca? My guess he's some tin-pot outlaw. By the time he tracks those horses we'll be long gone. Anyhow, there's a way to cover our tracks — or at least make it harder for this Barca to blame us for killing his men. How about we bury those fellas as you blew to hell back there and act like we know nothing about them?'

Joe nodded. 'Mmm . . . that might work. It's certainly worth a try. If we're going to do it then I guess we better get started.'

It was a gruesome business as they heaped the broken bodies in one place. They packed the saddles and spare weapons alongside the bodies. Joe placed the sack of dynamite in the grave.

'I reckon we won't need this now we got ourselves properly armed.'

It took considerable effort and time to cover the grisly remains with loose boulders in order to make a passable rocky tomb for the dead bandits.

'Shouldn't we say a prayer or something?' Butch queried.

'Do you know any prayers?'

Butch thought for a moment or two before replying,

'I don't reckon so, but I was thinking these here Mexicans believe in stuff like that.'

'We can make up some words,' Joe offered. 'You're good at that sort of thing . . . words, I mean.'

'Yeah, I guess.' Butch joined his hands together and looked up towards the sky. 'You know, I reckon it won't be long till dark. We ought to be well away from this place afore nightfall.'

'What? You reckon these dead men will rise up and come haunting us?'

'Don't talk like that, Joe. It ain't respectful. It's the living I'm worried about. We could be caught between two forces — bandits and prison guards. The further away from this place the better for my liking.'

'Just say the goddamn prayer and then we can get on.'

'OK! OK! Just remember I ain't no preacher man.'

'Well, you've been with a preacher girl. You must have learned something from her.'

Butch glared at Joe but could think of no suitable reply so he bent his head in an attitude of humble obeisance.

'Dear God, these poor fellas were maybe misguided somewhat, Don't be too hard on them when they get to the pearly gates. It weren't an easy death getting the living daylights blowed out of them what with Joe Peters chucking dynamite. So maybe they deserve a break from You. May they rest in peace, in this rocky sepulchre, for ever and ever, amen.'

The burial concluded, they discussed the possibility of retracing their steps to recover the mounts they had ridden from the mine, which had fled from the scene of the dynamiting.

'I don't like leaving them,' Butch opined. 'More than likely they'll wander back to the mine. When that happens the prison guards will have a lead on us and the direction we're headed.'

'It ain't worth going back down the trail after them. Hell knows how far they'll have gone by now. If those mounts are heading back to the stables they'll just keep on going. We go after them, we'll just be wasting the head start we got on anyone coming after us.'

'I guess you're right, at that. Well, let's get going then.'

They secured the spare mounts with the rope the bandits had used to make the corral and set off.

13

Joe awoke and lay for a while staring up as the sky began to lighten and the coming day gilded the horizon. Last night he had fallen into an exhausted sleep as soon as they had stopped and made camp. He still felt drugged from sleep as he slowly raised his head and looked around him.

At first he couldn't make out what the dim shapes spaced around the camp signified. There was a small movement as someone struck a match and applied it to a smoke. The light in the sudden illumination from the match showed a bearded face. Joe slipped his hand up by his shoulder to where he had placed his holstered pistol. Stealthily he groped around, his hand encountering nothing but the bare ground. Slowly he brought his other hand up and felt around. There came a sinister chuckle from out of the darkness.

'You lose something, *gringo*?'

There was a sudden rush of movement from near by as Butch came awake and scrambled to his feet. A gunshot sounded and Butch stopped moving.

'Sit down, *gringo*, or the next bullet will be in your gut.'

Butch slowly sank back on his blankets.

'Jose, get a fire going,' the voice continued. 'I need coffee.'

'What the hell's going on?' Joe growled. 'We're peaceful travellers on our way south. What you fellas want with us?'

The bearded man walked into the range of the firelight as the flames took hold. Even in the unsteady glow Joe could make out the squat figure of a powerfully built man. His shoulders were broad and his arms bulged with muscle.

'If you are so peaceful, *gringo*, why

are you herding stolen horses?'

'What the hell you mean, stolen? We traded fair and square for them there nags.'

'*Sí, señor*, you traded the lives of my men for those horses. I am very sad you tell so much lies. I think you are very bad man indeed. You come into my country killing and stealing and lying.' The bearded man shook his head in disapproval and pursed his lips. 'Such crimes should not go unpunished.'

As the man was talking Joe was glancing around the camp. What he saw was not encouraging. The light was getting brighter as the sun crept higher and higher, revealing more clearly the predicament they were in. Armed men ringed the campsite. In appearance they were similar to the men they had encountered yesterday on the trail through the ravine.

'There must be some mistake. We're just travelling through and traded those mounts for silver what we got paid at the Los Pecos mine.'

Joe did not see the signal that the man by the fire must have given. A rifle butt thudded painfully into the side of his head.

'Aaargh!' Joe yelled. 'Fella, you better watch what you're doing to citizens of the United States of America. There are harsh laws to punish brigands. You could find yourself in jail facing a long prison sentence, or your neck stretched on the end of a rope.' Joe tried to sit up but was hit again.

'Just stay down, *gringo* while I decide how I am to kill you.'

The smell of the fresh coffee being brewed set up pangs of hunger in Joe's innards.

'I don't suppose there's any chance of a mug of that there coffee?' he asked.

'Why would I give coffee to a murderer? You deserve nothing but a slow and painful death and I, Ramos Barca, am expert in such matters.'

Butch, who had been quiet up till this point, suddenly spoke.

'Joe, I guess this is the end of the trail

for us. We've had some good times together. Somehow the fights we had stand out in my memory more so than anything else.'

'Fighting and drinking,' Joe replied. 'It's what we do best.'

It was the signal. Joe drove his fist up into the crotch of the man standing by him — the one who had clouted him on the head with his rifle. As the Mexican grunted and bent over Joe grabbed him and heaved. Rolling forward, he came to his feet and shoved the man towards the fire, where Barca was squatting, sipping his coffee.

Helplessly the bandit flailed his arms as he was propelled forward. There was sudden confusion when he cannoned into the men by the fire. Joe ran at the group and saw a hand holding a gun coming out of the tangle of limbs. He kicked out, caught the wrist and the weapon flew into the air. Then he was in amongst the cluster of bodies, giving them no chance to recover from his surprise attack.

Somewhere in the background he could hear men cursing in Spanish as they fought to subdue Butch. Then he became engrossed in his own fight as a rifle butt came out of the mêlée and cracked him on the shoulder.

Joe kicked and punched out at the bandits, cursing and yelling as he fought. The struggle was fast and furious. Joe hit out at faces and bodies as they swirled around in a mad frenzy of fighting. One man fell into the fire and screamed as he rolled frantically away from the searing flames.

Joe kicked another on the knee. As the man went down Joe brought up his own knee and smashed it in the bandit's face. Punches and kicks were raining down on Joe, but he stood like a colossus and took everything slung at him, while at the same time dealing out terrible punishment to the men he was grappling with. There was a whole battalion of bandits ranged against two and no matter how hard they fought the odds were always stacked against them.

A rifle butt smashed into the back of Joe's head. He saw stars, staggered and almost lost his balance. Someone cannoned into his legs and he was bowled over. Even as he went down he grabbed at an unidentifiable shape and head-butted. Then he was on the ground, rifle butts and boots pummelling and kicking him into unconsciousness.

· 14

When Joe woke up he felt stiff and constricted. He tried to flex his muscles. Nothing gave. He was in a rigid and unnatural position and he realized that his hands and ankles were tightly bound. He remembered the fight with the Mexican bandits and the battering he had taken as he subsided beneath the weight of numbers.

Slowly he opened his eyes and discovered he was lying on his belly. His face was swollen and painful. In fact, every part of him hurt. He tried to roll over and found he was fixed in such a way as to make this impossible. He swivelled his head and felt the rough rawhide noose around his neck. His feet were raised in the air and though he flexed his muscles something prevented him from straightening his legs.

Cautiously he turned his head and

caught sight of his partner. For a moment he studied Butch's posture, then realized that what he was seeing was a duplicate of how he himself had been trussed.

Butch's hands and feet had been lashed together. A noose encircled Butch's neck and the end of the rope that formed this noose was fastened to his feet and the legs bent to form a right angle at the knees. The feet were held in place by a rough framework made from branches and hammered into the earth to keep it rigid. Butch turned his head and stared back at Joe.

'You look a mess,' Joe commented, noting his partner's blood-encrusted features.

'The way you look, you'd never win no beauty contest yourself,' Butch grunted, speaking with some difficulty through bruised and swollen lips. 'You look like a turkey that's been plucked and stuffed ready for a thanksgiving dinner.'

'It sure as hell feels like that. I can't

move sideward, upward or downward.'

Behind them they could hear the sounds of men at breakfast, as mugs rattled and spoons scraped over tin plates.

'You think we'll get breakfast?' Joe asked.

But Butch had other thoughts on his mind as he studied his partner's bindings.

'I got an uneasy feeling about this, Joe. I reckon I seen something like this afore, I mean the way we're trussed up like this.'

'You ain't going to tell me they're cannibals. We're to be roasted and fried with chilli beans? Hell, that don't seem no fittin' end for a man!'

'No, what happens is we choke ourselves to death.'

'That's right, *gringo*.'

Neither of the men had heard Barca come up on them. The bandit chief gave a signal and his men came up to Joe and pulled his elbows apart. They had brought sharpened stakes and drove these into the earth between the crook of Joe's elbow and his body. They repeated the same procedure on the other arm. Another two men were doing the same to Butch.

'You see, *gringo*, when I release your feet you won't be able to roll to one side or the other, but must remain in the one position. Then, *gringo*, we will see how long you last as you try to keep your feet in the air.'

Joe began to see the ingenuity of the plan. As his legs grew tired his feet would gradually lower to the ground and the attached noose would tighten and gradually strangle him.

The Mexicans made some adjustments to his bonds and he was pulled in a tight arc, his chest stretched tight as he rested on his belly. The taut posture was painful as his spine bent at an unnatural bowed manner.

'Goddamn you to hell, Barca!' Joe grunted as he felt the strain pulling on his muscles.

The bandit leader laughed.

'I am sorry I cannot stay to watch you die, *gringo*. I have other more pleasurable business to attend to. You should be grateful to me for letting you die so slowly. As you choke to death you will be able to consider your sins and repent. God is merciful, they tell me.

'If you are sincerely repentant, he might just let you get into heaven. But I fear you have killed many people, so maybe he will send you to hell for your wickedness. *Adios, gringo*.'

The bandit walked away. As he went there came the sound of mallets hammering and the framework holding Joe's feet up was knocked away. Joe immediately felt the noose tightening. He gasped as he tried to bring his legs back to their original position.

For long moments he stayed still, feeling the tension on his muscles as he strained to keep his legs upright.

'Goddamn!' he swore.

There were sounds of men readying their mounts, then the vibration of many hoofs on the earth as the bandits vacated the campsite. The sounds seemed to linger for a long time after the last of the horses had left.

'Joe, how are you?' Butch's voice was tense as he called to his partner.

'Goddamn!' Joe swore again. His legs slipped a fraction and the noose tightened. 'Goddamn slithering swine! When I catch up with that blasted Barca I'm going to pound his head into mince and feed it up his ass.'

The rawhide slipped another inch and the noose bit into Joe's neck. He stopped talking. He could feel his muscles trembling as he tensed them in an effort to keep his legs in an upright position. There was silence as the tension in their bodies grew and the agony in muscles increased.

'This is devilish, Joe. I think I'm getting cramp. Any ideas?'

'Think about something else; anything to take your mind off this. What about that preacher's daughter back awhile? Was she worth the running and the prison and now this?'

'Hell, ain't no woman worth strangling for.' There was a pause. 'The danged puzzle of it is, I would do it all over again.'

Joe wanted to laugh but held himself in. It would not help in his present predicament.

'Hell, Butch! You'll never change.'

'You think this is the end of the line?'

The strain was intolerable. Joe tried to keep still but his muscles let him down and the noose tightened another fraction. There was no more talk as they fought to keep the tension off the rawhide around their necks. Joe's feet dropped another notch. He tried to bring them back up again. It was difficult to breathe now. The noose tightened. He wanted to say goodbye to Butch but when he tried to speak only a gasping breath emerged. Then his legs gave out. The full weight of his feet dropped and the noose cut off his air.

Joe's mouth was wide open as he tried to breathe. His vision turned red, then black. He desperately wanted to live if only to kill the man who had put him here . . .

'Joe . . . I . . . don't think . . . I can . . . hold out . . . much longer . . . '

But there was no one listening and then there was no one talking.

15

Matias Romero was a goatherder. His job was to take his little flock of goats up into the hills to find pasture, and to protect them from wolves and coyotes and rustlers. Matias was ten years old and small for his age. He made up for his small stature by the brightness and cunning of his mind. Also Matias had a knife. It was a big knife and he kept it bright and shiny, using a stone to keep the edge sharp.

When he heard the horses moving through the passes he moved his little herd quickly into the corner of the meadow where they had been grazing. Satisfied that the goats were safe, he climbed up a tall rock to observe the horsemen. He drew in a sharp breath.

'Barca!' he hissed.

Matias had good reason to hate Barca, for the bandit chief robbed his way through the mountains. The boy had watched the bandits as they rode through and wished he could get close enough to plunge his knife into the black heart of their hated leader.

Leaving his little herd safely penned, Matias backtracked the horses. It was the boy's habit to forage in abandoned campsites; sometimes he would find treasures. It was in one such camp that he had found his precious knife. Soon he could smell wood smoke. He hurried forward, then stopped and stared at the bizarre sight of the two trussed men.

Matias crept closer. Here was a find indeed. His quick young mind worked out immediately what was happening. He saw the rawhide nooses and knew what needed to be done. But perhaps the men were past help. Matias pulled out his sharp knife and stepped forward.

The face of the bigger of the two men was red and mottled and his tongue hung out of his mouth. His eyes were closed and Matias believed he was dead already. Nevertheless he severed the tightened rawhide which had become partially buried in the man's neck. He could not help but draw blood. The man's arched body collapsed to the ground and a mighty sigh escaped from his gaping mouth.

Matias hurried to the second man and performed the same operation. When the noose was cut away this man opened his eyes and stared dazedly at Matias. He put his hands to his neck and began to massage the angry weals made by the tightened rawhide.

'Thank you,' he whispered hoarsely. Then he tried to stand, failed and crawled the few feet to his friend.

'Joe,' he said, in that strange, hoarse whisper.

Matias watched as the freed man began to slap and pummel the unconscious one.

'Joe,' Butch uttered the name hoarsely, unable to raise his voice above a whisper. 'Joe, talk to me, you big lummox. Don't die now and leave me all alone to find that bastard bandit and tear his evil heart out.'

Matias was gladdened to hear these sentiments. It was good to know he had undone Barca's wickedness and rescued men who were enemies of the bandit chief. He began a search of the camp. As he scavenged he could hear the men talking in that strange whispery way and he knew the bigger man had also revived.

Something shiny in the dirt caught his attention. He dug his fingers in to find a rowel that had become detached from a spur. After more searching he found a pan with a hole in it and a small tin of matches. He was quite pleased with his finds and turned back to the men he had rescued. They were sitting in the dirt observing his activities.

'Howdy kid,' the first man whispered. 'You got any water?'

'*Sí, señor*, but it is where I keep my goats. I must get back to them. Follow me.'

Wearily the men struggled to their feet. For a moment the boy watched them, but they made no effort to gather up the rawhide that had bound them so Matias coiled it and slung it over his shoulder. He retraced his steps back to his goats, the men following him obediently.

The progress was slow for the men had to stop from time to time and lean on each other. Now and then they cursed in those strange, hoarse voices, and said what they would do to Barca when they caught up with the bandit chief. But Matias did not think they meant any of it. These men were obviously too stupid to gain any advantage over Barca.

Matias had a goatskin water bag concealed where the sun would not warm it. He handed this over to the *gringos*. They sat beside him on the grass and sipped water, from time to time massaging the ugly weals where the rawhide had cut into their flesh.

'You saved our lives, little one. What is your name?'

Matias felt himself standing an inch or two taller when the man said this.

'Matias Romero.' He showed them the knife. 'I cut the rawhide with this. Was it Barca that tied you up?'

'*Sí*, Matias. You know this Barca?'

The boy's face contorted with hate. 'One day when I am old enough I will stick this fine knife in Barca's rotten heart and slit his throat.'

It seemed to Matias that the men looked at him with renewed respect.

'I'm sure glad you won't be coming after me with that there knife,' said the bigger of the men. 'I'd never sleep easy in my bed.'

Matias looked at him keenly to discern whether the man was making fun of him, but his eyes remained serious.

'We thank you, Matias Romero, for our lives. My name is Joe Peters, and this squirt here is Butch Shilton. Is there somewhere we could find shelter and food?'

'*Sí*, Señor Joe and Señor Butch. Help me round up my goats and I will take you to my village.'

16

Though the villagers had little to give, they shared it with the two strangers who had suddenly appeared in their midst.

'Goddamn it, Joe but we have arrived in paradise!' Butch opined one morning.

The hot sun beat down but the two men were shaded from the worst of the heat by a large mesquite. They were sitting at a table having a meagre breakfast of tortilla and beans.

'Butch, these people have nothing. They scratch a living from the fields and hills around them. They have to hide their food and their young women from Barca and his bandits. Even the men are not safe. He steals their food and their women and their men and they are helpless to stop him. Just because you've shacked up with that young widow woman don't make this no paradise.'

'Hell! I know that as well as you. Anyway, I have to stay somewhere and Dolores had a room vacant. It just seemed logical for me to hang my hat in her place. Anyway, she ain't no widow. Her husband was taken by Barca and forced to join his gang. She needs looking after.'

'That's even worse. What if her husband returns? How will that look if he finds his wife's taken up with another man?'

'It ain't what you think, Joe. It's just your low imagination making out a simple arrangement of convenience to be something it ain't. Anyway, if her husband is riding with Barca it ain't likely he'll return.

'It seems to me, Joe, as this could be a Garden of Eden, but that serpent Barca has snuck in and poisoned everything in it. Someone needs to tie a knot in his tail. There has to be some way of stopping him. How about you and me putting our heads together and coming up with a plan to rid the world of one lousy bandit?'

'You and me? I asked Matias how many men Barca has. He reckons around fifty. Hell, Butch! We would need an army to take him on.'

'I don't know, Joe. There's got to be a way. I've been thinking. How about we make a trip back to that grave where we buried those fellas you killed and recover the guns and ammo we stashed? Then we could arm the men of the village and give them a chance to fight back against Barca.'

'Stop right there. I don't mind the bit about recovering the guns but as for taking on Barca, it's a sure way of getting ourselves killed. I've no doubt that that Mexican bandit has many more unpleasant ways of butchering us. Don't forget, if it hadn't been for that kid Matias we'd have been buzzard meat.'

'Yeah, well, I just don't like the idea of sitting round here waiting for that slimy greaser to pounce again. Next time we might not survive.'

'Hell! You think I don't feel the same?' Joe sighed deeply. 'There's not a day goes by but I'm racking my brains to find some way of getting back at the man who tried to kill me in such a filthy manner. Shoot me, knife me, beat me to death but strangle me? That was one vile trick.'

'Yeah, I know what you mean. Anyway, we're going to need weapons of some sort no matter what happens, seeing as Barca took the guns we liberated from them dead bandits. So we need to go back to that grave and dig up some more of those guns. Armed, at least we stand a fighting chance against Barca and his gang.'

'I guess you're right, Butch, though it'll be a hell of a trek with no horses. Then we got to pack everything back here again,'

'Tomorrow — or as they say here, *mañana* — we'll set out early. Matias usually leaves with his goats just after dawn, so we'll travel part of the way with him. It'll probably take us a couple of days there and then a couple of days back. What you say?'

'Agreed, pard. Let's do it.'

Next morning Matias led them back to the campsite where they had been left to die. They carried water and a small amount of jerky made from goat meat.

'Good luck, *amigos*. Watch out for Barca.'

The warning was unnecessary. Butch and Joe were all too aware of the danger. They knew they had to proceed very carefully until they had once again armed themselves.

Because they were on foot it took most of the day to reach their destination. Cautiously they approached the site where they had interred the dead bandits. They looked dubiously at the pile of rocks they had stacked on top of the bodies.

'Those fellas are going to smell a mite ripe when we start pulling at them there rocks,' Butch said uneasily.

'Yeah, I know. However, if I recall, we buried the guns close to that wall of rock so maybe we won't have to disturb them.'

The smell from the decomposing bodies was so bad that the pair had to take numerous breaks as they worked. However, it was as Joe had said, and they were able to recover the guns they were seeking, along with the dynamite, without having to disturb the bodies. Except for a coating of dust the guns seemed none the worse for their brief burial. Butch strapped on a pair of pistols.

'Hell Joe! I feel dressed once more.'

Joe found an Army Colt .45 and a holster and was examining the rifles. He chose a Remington repeater and worked the mechanism.

'Well, maybe we might stand a slight chance against that skunk of a bandit chief now we are properly armed. But we got to stay alert. One of us will always have to be on guard while the other rests or sleeps.'

'I guess I don't want to go through that ordeal for a second time.' Butch rubbed his neck where the red marks of the rawhide noose were still evident. 'If Barca catches us again with our britches down he'll make sure he finishes us. When we do meet up, this time I aim to make him regret ever tangling with us.'

Just then they heard the horses coming up the trail.

17

It was a mad scramble to get under cover. Butch dived to one side of the trail while Joe went for the opposite side. They waited. The horsemen seemed to be in no hurry; the hoof-beats sounded slow but steady. The ambushers lay low, anxiously watching the trail for sight of the riders. Then Butch cursed long and low.

'Goddamn it, Joe! The sack of dynamite is lying there as plain to see as . . . as . . . a naked woman.'

In his haste to go to ground Joe had left the dynamite lying on the track. Whoever came up the trail past the grave would see the bulging sack. It might alert them sufficiently either to scare them off or provoke them into starting a shooting match with Joe and Butch the unwilling targets. Then it was too late to retrieve the sack. The horses came into view.

Butch knew instinctively that they had been rumbled. The horses were without riders. It was evident that their masters, suspecting something was amiss, had dismounted and allowed the mounts to carry on in order to distract the ambushers, leaving their riders to sneak up on whoever was lying in wait for them.

Joe and Butch lay there, eyes scanning the trail, ears straining for a noise that would warn them of the start of the impending attack. The horses came on and, scenting the two men, stopped. One came over to where Butch was lying and stood patiently staring down at him.

'Git!' Butch hissed.

But the horse stood there, blinking and watching him, making snuffling noises and chewing its bit. Butch stared anxiously up the trail.

'You see anything, Joe?' he called in a low voice.

'Hell no! Nothing.'

'Me neither.'

The horse moved closer and Butch turned impatiently, about to strike out with his pistol if necessary to drive the animal away. Suddenly he paused. With a critical eye he examined the harness and the saddle. The leathers were worn and shabby. A suspicion was slowly forming in Butch's mind.

'Joe.'

'Yeah? You see something?'

'What I see is our two missing mounts.'

'You what?'

'I suspicion these are the horses we were riding that day we were ambushed, the ones as we got from the silver mine.'

'Goddamn! Butch, are you sure?'

'I reckon they are the goddamn horses we rode up here. When you set off the dynamite they spooked and took off. They been wandering around here ever since.'

'You said they would run all the way back to the mine.'

'Seems to me as these here horses ain't trail wise. All they know is working in that there mine. Without someone to take care of them they're lost.'

'The thing is — are they alone or what?'

'Only one way to find out; walk up that trail and see if someone shoots your fat head off.'

'After you, Butch. It was your idea.'

Cautiously, Butch stood up. The horses waited patiently. Butch took hold of a bridle and began walking back up the trail, leading the animal. In spite of his belief that the horses were alone he couldn't help wondering if someone was indeed drawing a bead on him as he walked. Nothing happened and he breathed a sigh of relief.

'It looks as if we got our horses back. That certainly makes the journey back to the village a lot easier. I'm sure goddamn tired of all that walking.'

Joe moved out of hiding and patted his mount.

'You and me both. Let's get them

loaded up with these spare guns and start back.'

'We got guns, rifles and pistols and ammunition and dynamite. You reckon we could take on Barca and teach that sonabitch it was a mistake to mess with us?'

Joe nodded reluctantly. 'Something like that. Though we have to persuade the men in that village to help. Hell, Butch! They're nothing but farmers. Probably the only thing they ever shot is a rabbit — and I doubt even that. I ain't seen any sign of a firearm all the time we been holed up there. I can't see them going against hardened fighters like Barca's gang. That leaves us two against fifty. I can think of easier ways to commit suicide.'

'There's another way to fight Barca.'

Joe turned and looked at his partner, his eyes squinting against the hot sun.

'What we lack are men,' Butch went on, 'fighting men, to take on Barca and his bandits. Right now there's just me and you and those farmers.'

'It's one sure thing; those farmers back at that village ain't no fighters,' Joe agreed. 'They do what farmers do best: raise crops and kids.'

'This might be a break we didn't foresee. If these dumb horses didn't go back to the mine then the guards wouldn't have been able to backtrack. That gives me an idea. I know this might sound crazy, but tell me, where are there plenty of fighting men — or at least dangerous men — who would put up a show against Barca?'

The big man tightened a cinch while he thought about it, then shook his head.

'I give up. Where?'

'Los Pecos,'

Joe's head came round and he stared at Butch.

'Los Pecos?' he echoed.

'Tough men, hard men, men who might jump at the chance to take up a gun and fight for a chance at freedom.'

'Jeez! Butch, that is one crazy idea.

There are several things against it. Firstly Los Pecos is a prison. It's got a stockade and armed guards to keep them convicts safely penned in. Secondly, the men in there are criminals — cut-throats and killers, not much better than Barca himself. And thirdly, how are we to recruit anyone from there when we are escapees ourselves? As soon as we show our faces anywhere near there we'll be hung, drawn and quartered.'

'We don't go anywhere near the prison. We go to the mine and we free a batch of prisoners. Then we bring them back to the village and arm them. When Barca turns up to forage for food and recruits we're lying in ambush. We shoot the living daylights out of him and his gang of brigands.'

'Butch, it is a crazy idea. In all the time I knowed you, you've come up with some harebrained schemes but this has got to be the most stupid, idiotic, ridiculous, wild idea you've ever had.' Joe looked up at the sun. 'How long you think it'll take us to get to the mine?'

18

It was approaching nightfall when they arrived in the vicinity of the silver mine. They hid the horses in a patch of mesquite and made their way on foot to the outskirts of the mine workings.

'I say we walk through this place as if we had every right to be here. The chances of someone recognizing us are pretty remote. The first gang of convicts we come across we take out the guards and vamoose pretty damn quick.'

'What about those leg-irons? Those fellas won't be able to run with chains on and we won't have time to break them.'

'You're right. We need a wagon. Pile them all on the wagon and hightail it back to the village.'

The two men looked at each other. Suddenly they grinned.

'It'll take a lot of luck to pull this off.'

'I guess you're right, but hell! We done harder than this in the past.'

Spontaneously each raised a hand towards the other. They slapped palms together.

'Good luck, pardner!'

Once again the pair visited the stables and selected two horses that looked as if they might be able to stand up to a journey back to the village. There was plenty of harness to tack up the horses and when they were ready they led them outside.

No one took any notice of the two men threading their way through the cluster of mining buildings with a couple of horses. Such a spectacle was normal enough not to arouse comment.

When they got to the area of the mine workings the noise of the crusher was ear-numbing. Five prisoners were loading rocks on to the continuous belt that climbed unremittingly up to the maw of the crusher and tumbled the rocks into the belly of the beast, to be pulverized and washed for the silver content.

There were five men loading, with a guard watching over them. The guard was amusing himself by flicking his bull-whip at each of the men in turn, catching them on various parts of their bodies. With every strike the prisoners jerked with the sting of the rawhide. This was normal behaviour for the warders, who were invariably sadistic by nature and whiled away the tedium of guard duty by abusing the men in their charge.

So engrossed was this guard in harassing his charges that he took no notice of the men leading in the horses. Butch headed over to where a couple of wagons were parked and indicated for Joe to harness up. Then he turned and walked towards the workforce labouring and sweating under a dying sun.

Butch realized that they had to be quick, for the shift would be ending soon and the men working underground would be coming up to the surface. He and Joe had to be on their way before that happened.

The first thing that made the guard realize something was amiss was the appearance of the pistol pointed at his belly. His hand twitched towards his own weapon. Butch shook his head and raised his pistol so that the guard should not mistake his intention. He signalled the guard to turn around. With the racket of the crusher there was no possibility of vocal communication. With a snarl and a threat that was lost in the noise the guard did as he was told. Butch removed the man's pistol and transferred it to his own waistband.

The prisoners, realizing something out of the ordinary was happening, were glancing up warily at the man in the sombrero. Butch kept his gun on the guard, waiting until Joe had brought up the wagon. Then, after motioning to Joe to keep the guard covered, Butch used the whip to bind the man's hands. Then he tipped him to the ground. So far the whole operation was going smoothly.

Butch strode over to the prisoners, who had now ceased work and were observing his activities with keen interest. He was vaguely disappointed to see that there were only five prisoners, but he knew he could not push his luck by waiting for more to be brought up from underground. The convicts would not be alone but would be accompanied by guards. There would be every possibility of Butch and Joe having a fight on their hands.

Using signs, he urged the five men towards the wagon, pointing vaguely towards the distant hills to indicate that they would soon be free. They immediately grasped the essential idea that this was a rescue operation and shuffled forward, trailing their chains, eager to clamber aboard the wagon. Butch heaved a sigh of relief and kept glancing every now and then towards the mine entrance. When he looked again at the wagon he frowned. Only four men were on board.

'Damnit to hell! Where'd that other fella get to?'

No one answered as there was such a din from the machinery that no one could hear him. He glanced back at the crusher and saw the missing prisoner. The rescued man had gone to the trussed-up guard, had picked up a piece of rock and was now raising it above his head.

'No!' Butch yelled. He lurched towards the convict. The guard, seeing what was coming, tried to twist away. It was useless. Thirty pounds of jagged rock smashed into the side of his head with such force that his skull was cracked open like an eggshell. Blood and brains spilled out. Such was the bile and hatred roused in the convict that he brought up the rock to strike again. In any case it would have been overkill for the man was already dead. No one could have survived that initial brutal blow.

Butch cannoned into the convict as

he was about to repeat his action. The man overbalanced and the rock fell from his hands. His face was contorted with rage and hatred and he was mouthing curses.

Butch grabbed the convict by the shirt, attempting to drag him away from the crusher with the intention of getting him into the wagon. He was sickened and shocked by the brutal slaying of the guard and felt in some way responsible, for he had bound the man, leaving him helpless and unable to defend himself.

'Get in that goddamn wagon afore I use that rock to pound *your* brains out,' he yelled.

The killer swung a roundhouse at him. Butch tried to sidestep to avoid the blow. He only partly succeeded for his foot trod on the bloody head of the dead guard. Butch went down and the convict aimed a kick at him. Seething with anger, Butch grabbed the foot and heaved with all his considerable strength. His action had unexpected results.

His attacker grabbed wildly at the crusher as he overbalanced. Butch saw the convict's mouth open as he yelled something. Then the man was rising up along the frame of the rumbling belt.

Butch reckoned the convict was trying to escape him by riding the belt out of his reach. He jumped up and grabbed the man around the waist. It was of no avail; the convict's grip on the conveyor was secure. Still holding on to the convict, Butch was being hoisted upward and the two men rose up along the conveyor of the crusher.

'Goddamn it!' Butch yelled into the noise. 'Let go!'

Then Butch saw why the man was not relinquishing his grip: he wasn't *holding* on, his arm was trapped in the conveyor. Slowly the two men were pulled higher and higher as the belt shuddered and growled inexorably upwards.

'Turn the goddamn thing off!' Butch yelled, hoping someone down below would see what was happening and come to his aid.

He might as well have sneezed for all the good it did him. The watchers below could only speculate that Butch was trying to recapture the escaping man. From the ground, there was no way of telling it any other way. So they waited and watched the struggle and wondered if Butch would win the fight to bring his man down to earth again.

19

Butch felt the convict's body wriggling as he struggled to free his arm. He was yelling something at the same time. Butch tried to move his hold and clamber higher over the trapped man in an attempt to assist him. A fist came round and punched him on the ear. Butch almost lost his grip as he slipped. His hands grabbed desperately, one finding a grip on the man's britches while the other reached out for a hold on the conveyor.

The convict was trying to free his arm and at the same time rid himself of Butch. His wildly kicking foot hit Butch in the face.

'Goddamn!' Butch yelled. When the boot came round a second time he instinctively put out a hand to block the kick. At the same time he lost his grip.

He grabbed frantically at the side of

the conveyor belt. Another powerful kick from the convict sent him backwards out into space. Yelling wildly, Butch crashed to earth with a jolt that knocked the wind out of him.

'Goddamn!' he wheezed feebly, staring up at the struggling convict. Then the man went over and into the crusher.

Butch stared in disbelief at the empty space where the man had been one moment and in the next had disappeared into the maw of that brutal machine designed to crush rocks.

If the doomed convict screamed no one could hear him above the roar of the machine that was pulverizing his body into mincemeat. Butch closed his eyes and shuddered.

A hand grabbed his shoulder. Butch punched out instinctively before looking; when he did look he saw Joe Peters's irate face glaring down at him.

Joe's mouth was working as he yelled something. Butch sat up, dazedly looking around him, then noticed the wagon moving off as the remaining convicts made good their escape.

'Goddamn it, Joe! Would you look at that. Stop those mad bastards before someone else does.'

Joe looked at where Butch was pointing, then turned and ran after the wagon. Butch groaned as he struggled to his feet and felt the pain throbbing through his bruised and battered body.

'Goddamn!' he yelled in frustration. 'What a goddamn mess!'

He had been lying beside the dead guard. For a moment he looked with pity at the crushed skull, shaking his head at the utter senselessness of the killing. With sudden foresight he realized that the first people out of the mine would raise the alarm as soon as they saw the body of the murdered guard. With abrupt resolution he grabbed the dead guard under the arms and heaved him on to the belt, which was still rumbling away with no one to attend it and no one to load it. For a moment he watched the body being trundled towards the top of the moving belt.

'Sorry, my friend,' he muttered. 'That might just delay discovery.' When he looked for his partner, Joe was out of sight. 'Hell damnit! This is turning into disaster.'

Muttering curses he hobbled in the direction in which he had last seen Joe and the wagon.

Joe had caught up with the escaping convicts. Luckily no one had observed the wagon being driven by a bunch of manacled men or the alarm would certainly have been raised.

When Butch eventually arrived on the scene Joe was waiting for him, holding the convicts at the point of a gun. Butch decided the best course was for the prisoners to sit peacefully in the body of the wagon; anyone noticing them would, hopefully, believe that they were being transported to another job within the mining compound. While Butch clambered into the driver's seat Joe sat in the back along with the convicts, keeping his gun in plain sight.

'I'm Joe Peters, and that's Butch Shilton driving this here wagon. You might recall we escaped from Los Pecos.'

'Hell, are you them two fellas? The prison was a misery after you broke out. It was bad enough before, but then we were put on short rations while they grilled us to say where you had gone. Nobody knew nothing. Why've you come back, anyhow?'

The four surviving convicts were a mixed crew. There was one black man amongst them. He was very dark, with matted curly hair and features that looked like rawhide stretched over a skull. An older man, with a full head of dark hair and a perpetual leer on his face, made a contrast with his pasty-skinned, smooth features. There were two younger men, probably in their early twenties but looking older, maybe because of the rough life they had led.

Joe began explaining the reasons for the rescue. Well, not everything. He failed to tell them about Barca and his fifty-strong gang.

'We need some men for a job we aim to complete. You fellas just qualified for the position.'

Butch was driving steadily as they talked; soon the mining compound was left behind.

'What's this job entail?' the oldest of the men enquired.

'We'll tell you more when we're safely away from here. When they find that dead guard they're bound to come after us.'

'Won't find no dead guard,' Butch called. 'I tossed him into the crusher to join that fella as killed him.' Butch was shaking his head. 'What the hell he want to go and do a thing like that for, sure beats me.'

'That was Jeff Kouts. Never was right in the head. Kill a man as soon as look at him. Mean through and through. He ain't no loss, neither.'

'Well, no matter. We sure could have used him if he'd behaved.'

They reached the place where they

had hobbled their own horses. They tied them to the rear of the wagon and continued onwards with the same arrangement: Joe riding inside with his gun on the convicts and Butch driving. All the time they kept looking over their shoulders at their back trail, wondering how long it would be, before a posse came chasing after them.

20

The fugitives travelled all that evening and well into the night, Butch guiding the wagon and steering by the stars. The convicts, like men everywhere who have surrendered control of their lives to others, curled up in the bottom of the wagon and went to sleep. Joe kept nodding off from time to time, only to jerk awake with a guilty start.

Dawn was just edging up into the morning sky by the time they reached the site of the original camp where Barca had surprised them and trussed them with such deadly purpose. Butch reined in and sat in the driving seat for some moments, trying desperately not to close his eyes and fall asleep. His body ached all over and he was sore from sitting on the hard, wooden seat as the wagon jolted and rumbled over a trail that was not really a trail, only a route he knew they had to travel to get to their destination.

'Butch, you OK?' asked Joe.

The convicts were stirring now that the wagon's movement had ceased. Slowly they raised themselves up and stared with sleep-dulled eyes at their surroundings.

'What hell-hole is this you've brought us to?' one asked sourly.

Butch clambered down from the wagon and stood stretching, trying to ease the stiffness from his aching body.

'We take a break here,' Joe told the men.

'What about breakfast?'

'Ain't no breakfast yet. We got a mite further to go afore you get fed.'

'Fella, you better tell us where you taking us, else we ain't going nowhere.'

'First off tell us your names and what you did to land you in Los Pecos penitentiary.'

'Josh Killick,' one of the younger convicts answered. He was a robust youngster, with a mop of dark, unruly hair. 'I robbed a few banks is all, until I got caught.'

'George Stanton,' the other youngster contributed. 'Josh and I rode together. We were caught at the same time.'

'Damian Fakenham,' the oldest of the men offered, 'embezzlement and fraud.'

'Aaron Charles,' the black man was the last to speak, 'stole a pig.'

'What? You got sent to Los Pecos for stealing a goddamn Pig?'

Aaron shrugged. 'It were a white man's pig.'

Joe and Butch were staring at him. The black man shrugged his lean shoulders once more.

'My family were starving. I stole the pig, killed it and ate it.'

Fakenham started laughing. 'Serve you right for murdering a pig.'

The black man glared at Fakenham. 'I'd do the same to you, only I wouldn't feed you to my dog, you're too mean and sour.'

'Shut your mouth! Have some respect for your betters.'

Aaron closed his lips tight and said nothing.

'Well, now we all introduced, let me tell you why we've sprung you from Los Pecos,' Butch began. 'Since breaking out of prison we . . . '

'You killed a guard,' Stanton interrupted him. 'Isaac Devlin, and buried him in the cesspit.'

'Hell! It was an accident,' Butch riposted, 'He fell in there and drowned.'

'Try telling that to his brother. He got a posse made up of his family and they're out there hunting you right now.'

Butch and Joe exchanged uneasy glances.

'Well, they must be hunting in all the wrong places, for we ain't seen hide nor hair of them.'

'Then what you want us for?'

'There's a village not far from here and it's full of ordinary farmers and women and children. Then there's this here bandit fella, name of Barca, as is bleeding that village dry. He comes in

148

with his gang and takes what he wants ? food and women and recruits for his gang. The people live in fear of his raids. He comes and goes as he pleases and takes what he wants.

'Well, Joe and me, we intend stopping this galoot. We were hoping as you fellas would join us and help us fight Barca and his gang.'

There was silence as Butch's audience digested this information. Then a voice said: 'You want us to fight these goddamn bandits? What are these villagers paying?'

Butch had the grace to look a mite uncomfortable before he replied:

'They ain't paying nothing. They got nothing to pay. Over the years Barca has taken all their wealth. They're poor and miserable and helpless against these bandits and right now we're their only hope.'

'So . . . so what do we get out of the deal?' Fakenham sounded genuinely puzzled.

'A chance to redeem yourself for

your past misdeeds and gain your freedom.'

Fakenham looked at Butch with an incredulous expression on his face.

'You're one crazy son of a bitch if you expect us to believe that. Come on, tell the truth. These people have got hidden treasure or something. I hear there's Spanish gold buried hereabouts in these hills. I bet that's what it's all about, ain't it?'

For once Butch seemed to be lost for words. He stared at the ground, scuffing his boot in the dust.

'Ain't no use, Butch,' Joe called. 'We got to let them in on it. After all, there's plenty enough to go around.'

Butch looked up, his face impassive.

'We didn't want to say anything at this stage in case we all got to fighting each other over it, but Joe's right. There's enough to go around. When we get to the village I don't want anyone blabbing about no treasure. If the villagers get wind of our motives they'll vanish into the hills like they do when

Barca comes raiding.

'We go in there, defeat Barca, who's only there for the same reason we are. Once he's out of the way we can get our hands on the treasure and then we're all free to go our separate ways.'

'That's more like it,' Fakenham was nodding agreement. 'I'm in, then.' He glanced around at the other convicts. 'What about you fellas?'

Josh Killick and George Stanton nodded together. 'Yeah, we'll go along.'

Aaron Charles remained silent till Fakenham turned to him.

'What about you, fella? I guess you'd better strike out on your own. This ain't no place for no Negroes. This here is a white man's club.'

'I ain't hankering to be no part of no club that got scum like you in it.'

Aaron got no further as Fakenham made a dive for him. The older man took the black man by surprise and they both tumbled out of the wagon with Fakenham's hands locked around the other man's neck.

'Yippee!' Josh yelled. 'Go get him, Damien.'

He and George crowded to the side of the wagon to watch the fight.

Unfortunately for Fakenham, when he fell to the ground Aaron ended up on top. With a powerful heave of his forearms he broke Fakenham's grip on his throat and then smashed his fist into the white man's face.

'You dumb sonabitch,' Aaron yelled, 'I ain't taking that from no man.'

Fakenham screamed and flailed his arms in a vain attempt to dislodge his assailant. Aaron batted the man's arms to one side and hit him again. Blood was pouring from Fakenham's nose.

'Help me!' he yelled as he realized Aaron was no pushover. 'Get this black devil away from me!'

Joe moved in behind the struggling men and slipped his arms under Aaron's arms and brought his hands together behind the man's neck. It was a powerful grip and the convict was helpless as Joe pulled him up and away from Fakenham. Aaron struggled ineffectually as Joe held him.

'Let me go! That piece of trash needs to be taught a lesson.'

Once he was relieved of Aaron's weight, Fakenham rose to his feet and rushed at the helpless black man. He got one good blow in before Joe realized what was happening and swung his captive around and out of reach.

'Damnit all!' he roared, 'Will you fellas stop this fighting afore I get mad at you both.'

But Joe was wasting his breath. Fakenham kept coming after Aaron, swinging wild punches while Joe tried to keep the black man out of his reach.

'Oh, hell!' Joe snarled. He put his knee in Aaron's back, pushed him away, then turned and smashed Fakenham in the face. Fakenham went down and stayed down. Aaron, seeing the white man helpless, made an attempt to move around Joe and have another go at Fakenham but Joe had lost his temper by now.

He let go with a roundhouse that hit Aaron on the side of the head and the big black man staggered back, his feet tangled in his chains. He went down with a thump.

'Any more fighting and I'm going to bury both of you right here,' Joe yelled, staring furiously at the men on the ground, daring them to challenge him. The two downed men looked up at the big man standing over them with his fists clenched and stayed where they were.

'Hell! I had enough, boss,' Aaron grunted. 'Just keep that piece of white trash away from me or you'll be one man short.'

21

Fakenham stood, wiping at the blood on his face and glaring at Aaron.

'There's one thing for certain: you won't be going home with no treasure, fella,' he snarled. 'You'll be dead.' Fakenham rattled the chain of his manacles and looked up at Joe. 'When do we get rid of these?'

Joe was breathing heavily, still mad at the two fighters.

'All in good time,' he growled. 'I've a mind to put the goddamn chain around your neck an' stop up your talking and fighting for good and all.'

Fakenham stared sullenly back at him but dropped his eyes as the big man glared belligerently. Joe turned around and espied Butch leaning against the side of the wagon, watching his pardner's antics.

'And you were a big help, Shilton.'

'Hell, Joe! I thought you had everything in hand. You were having such a whale of a time, I didn't want to spoil your fun.'

'Why the hell I ever agreed to this harebrained scheme sure beats me. It's been nothing but trouble, since we went back to that mine for this bunch of troublemakers.'

Butch straightened up from the side of the wagon.

'Right, you fellas,' he said. 'Here's the deal. When we get to the village there'll be tools to break those chains. Once you're free of them there chains then you're also free to leave. You'll get a gun and some provisions. The village is over the border so you can keep going deeper into Mexico, where there's less chance of getting caught again.

'Those that choose to stay will have a chance to do some good by ridding the world of these bandits and getting rich at the same time. Anyone got any questions?'

Nobody spoke. Butch continued:

'OK, we're all tired after a night with no sleep. We have a mite more to go so I suggest you conserve your energy for getting there. I need someone to drive this damn wagon. My ass feels as stiff as a dried-out buffalo hide and my eyes are burning like piss-holes in the sand. I need to curl up in the back of the wagon and get me some shut-eye.'

Aaron raised his hand.

'I'll drive the wagon. That way I won't have to look at this heap of chicken dung I've managed to drop myself in.'

'Why can't we have a gun now in case we run into trouble?' Fakenham demanded. 'I feel naked out here without nothing to defend myself.'

'Don't give that murdering scum no gun,' Aaron objected. 'He's liable to shoot you in the back like the coward he is.'

'Nobody's getting no guns for now. For gawd's sake, can we just pull together for a change and stop this fighting? We're all in the same goddamn boat — or the same wagon. When we've defeated Barca you can shoot the hell out of each other for all I care. In fact you'd be doing the human race a favour. It'll be a few less, scum-encrusted crawfish left on the earth and maybe some people might sleep in their beds more easy at night with you lot six feet under.'

Joe decided to ride one of the horses behind the wagon and keep an eye on the convicts. Butch curled up to sleep while Aaron took up the reins.

'Hell!' Joe muttered to himself. 'You'd think they'd just be grateful to get out of that hell-hole and not fall to fighting at every opportunity.'

They had been travelling for some time when there was a sudden commotion ahead. Joe was jerked out of a doze and grabbed his .45. He peered up the trail to see what was happening.

'Señor Joe, Señor Joe..'

He recognized Matias standing by the side of the trail, waving frantically. Aaron pulled up the wagon alongside the boy and Matias ran to Joe's horse.

'Señor Joe, you can't go back. Barca is looking for you. It is terrible. He is burning the houses. He says he will return every day and burn more houses until the *gringos* are given up to him.'

Joe wanted to start swearing but the presence of the boy prevented him. Instead he climbed down from his horse and placed his hands on the youngster's shoulders.

'Slow down, young 'un. You are safe now, your Uncle Joe is here.'

By now Butch had awakened and was sitting up, rubbing the sleep from his eyes.

'What the hell's going on?'

The four convicts were twisting round in the wagon, curiously watching Joe and Matias.

'Señor Butch, it is terrible. Barca is raiding the village and setting fire to the houses. I hid from them and watched. Barca says he will take some of the people and kill them unless they hand over you and Señor Joe.'

'The hell you say! Joe, we got to get over there soonest, and stop this varmint once and for all. Dig out the guns and let these guys have what they want.'

'We can't go into a fight with these chains on,' Fakenham objected.

'OK, you stay here with the kid while we go on in without you.'

'I'm coming with you,' insisted Matias. 'Give me a gun. I can shoot,'

Aaron chuckled. 'Even the kid has more balls than you, Fakenham. What a yeller dawg you turned out to be. Whingeing and bellyaching is all you're good at.'

'Shut your black mouth afore I shut it for you.'

'All right, all right!' Butch was banging his hand on the side of the wagon. 'Both of you button your mouths. We got a mess of bandits down the road ready to massacre a village and you want to fight each other. I've a good mind to chain you both to a tree and leave you for the wolves to find.

Now stop your bitching and get hold of a weapon.'

Joe was unloading the arms they had excavated from the grave. Josh Killick and George Stanton jumped down from the wagon.

'Josh and me, we'll come with you.'

The two bank robbers shuffled up and grabbed a rifle apiece and a pistol.

'Weeeeh!' Josh yelled. 'It feels good to have a gun in my hands again.' He waved the pistol wildly in the air. 'Come on, Barca, you no-account varmint. I'm going to drill so many holes in you you'll look like a sieve.'

In his excitement he pulled the trigger and let off a shot.

'Goddamn it, that's right!' Butch raged. 'Let them know we're coming. Now we lost the element of surprise.'

'Sorry.'

Josh looked crestfallen while his partner George grinned at his discomfiture.

'No wonder we got caught robbing banks. I sure teamed up with one goddamn, bird-brained idiot,'

'Joe, I'll ride ahead. As soon as you get these . . . these loon-witted losers organized, follow on.'

Butch untied his horse from the wagon and mounted. Waving a hand in farewell he raced off down the trail. In a while he could smell the smoke of burning homes. He kept going, all the time on the lookout for Barca and his raiders.

22

Butch was too late. Barca had done his cruel work and was gone. The outlaw had not burned the entire village, as Butch had feared, but only torched a few of the hovels. Slowly, he rode into the village, the stink of burning fouling his nostrils. The villagers stared sullenly as he approached. They had been trying to rescue what they could from the burnt-out hovels. Now they ceased their labours and watched as the *gringo* rode into their midst. Slowly he dismounted.

'*Buenos dias.*'

No one responded to his greeting. Butch tied up his horse and walked to the smouldering ruins. Most of the dwellings in the village had been simple structures constructed from adobe with grass roofs. For this reason only the roofs burned when set alight but the effect on the dwelling was catastrophic.

The burning thatch collapsed into the home and set fire to any combustible materials within.

Butch turned to the villagers. 'I'm sorry,' he said. 'I brought some help. Maybe we can stop this sort of thing happening again.'

Their defeated faces stared back at him, then they averted their eyes.

'They never burned afore,' an old man with sparse whiskers said. 'Barca wants the *gringos*. We did not know where you were. He said he'd be back. If we do not hand you over, he would burn some more. Soon, he said, there would be no more houses left to burn.'

'How is this to end?' another man asked. 'Our village is half-dead already. When Barca comes back what can we do? We have nowhere else to go.'

'You *gringos* should leave. If you go, perhaps Barca will leave us alone. Life was hard before, but now it is a living hell.'

The speaker spread his arms, then

dropped them to his sides in a helpless gesture.

As he gazed round at the destruction and the still smoking homes Butch felt an impotent rage flare within him. These people were simple peasants. They had not the means to stand against the ruthless bandits that preyed on them; no way of fighting back.

Not knowing how to respond, Butch walked to his horse and fiddled with the saddle, adjusting what did not need adjusting. He was relieved when he spotted Joe approaching.

Joe was alone which worried Butch; he wondered where the convicts were. Joe waved, then turned in the saddle and beckoned to someone behind him. To Butch's relief the wagon with the convicts aboard hove into sight, Matias was sitting up in the driving seat beside Aaron.

'These people are not very happy with us, Joe,' Butch said as his partner pulled up beside him. 'They blame us for this burning.'

Slowly Joe dismounted. 'Hell damn that Barca! He has a lot to answer for. Well, let's get these fellas free from them chains and then we can worry about what to do next.'

The wagon with the escaped convicts pulled into the village, each side staring with curiosity at the other. The villagers were wondering what new woes were being visited upon them with the arrival of more *gringos*, the newcomers were taking in the smoking ruins and miserable appearance of the inhabitants.

'Hell, I once passed through a Texas town called Desolation,' Damien Fakenham offered. 'The place sure suited the name. I reckon this must be its sister town, Misery.'

'Let's get those chains off, and then see if we can help these poor people.'

It was while they were hammering at the leg irons the full extent of Barca's raid became known.

'Señor Joe, Señor Joe!' It was Matias with stricken face and tears in his eyes.

'They have taken the women.'

The boy stood before them, a picture of woe. Joe moved forward and gathered the boy in his arms.

'Matias, calm down, tell us what has happened.'

Between sobs the boy revealed the true malignity of the bandit chief. Normally the villagers had lookouts posted to warn of the bandits' approach but Barca had come on so swiftly that they had had no chance to prepare for the raid.

The tragic consequences of the surprise raid were that some of the females who would normally have had time to hide were taken unawares. Barca's men, delighted with this unexpected bonus, took five women with them when they rode from the village.

While Butch and Joe discussed this latest development and tried to formulate a plan to combat Barca, the escaped convicts were using borrowed tools to break free of their manacles.

'Joe, we gotta go after them. There's no telling what those devils will do to those women.'

'I guess you're right, pal.'

The pair stared grimly at each other. Then they began to question the villagers to find out in which direction the raiders had gone. They were hoping someone would know where the bandits' hideout was located.

So absorbed were they in these interrogations they were paying little attention to the actions of the convicts. They had only to look up and they would have seen the men they had freed, picking up weapons and staring balefully at them. When finally Joe did take notice, he gave a low grunt.

'Butch.'

'Yeah, what is it?' Butch followed Joe's gaze and went very still. Surrounding them were the four convicts, armed with the weapons he and Joe had supplied when they thought they would have to fight off the bandits attacking the village; four very dangerous men

were now aiming those same guns at
Joe and Butch.

23

'I wouldn't, mister.'

Butch's hand stopped moving. He glared with mounting anger and frustration at the array of guns holding Joe and himself at bay.

'You lousy, stinking polecats. We go to the trouble of springing you from that death-trap of a prison and you go and pull a trick like this.'

'Just do as you're told and we'll return the favour by not killing you. Unbuckle those gunbelts and toss them over here. Do it real careful, like. You make one wrong move and we start shooting.'

Reluctantly the two men unbuckled and let the leather belts fall to the ground.

'I said toss them over here,' snarled Fakenham. 'If you don't start obeying orders soon I'm going to put a bullet in you.'

Butch made to bend down for the discarded gunbelt but stopped abruptly when a shot rang out and a bullet buried itself in the dirt between his boots.

'Kick it over!' Fakenham yelled. 'You got a death wish or something? Any more tricks and the next bullet will be in your goddamn knee. The only reason you're still alive is because these fainthearts only agreed to jump you if you weren't going to be harmed. But that can soon change if you start acting stupid.'

'What about the treasure? You won't find it without our help.'

Fakenham chuckled. 'When we saw this village we knew there was no treasure. I never saw such a Godforsaken hole. You think these people would live like this if they had a Spanish treasure chest back of them. Nice try, Joe Peters, but this is one fella whose profession it was to con people out of their money and possessions. You can't con a conman. Now do as I say and kick those belts over here, *pronto*.'

There was nothing for it. They hooked the belts on to their boot toes and swung them over towards the convicts.

'Collect up them there guns, Aaron. We're cutting out of here *pronto*.'

'You want those guns, Fakenham, you pick them up yourself. I ain't no white man's slave. Pres Lincoln tol' me so himself. He had a lotta men killed to set me free.'

Fakenham's face went white; his expression tautened in anger. For a moment it was touch and go whether he would turn his gun on the black man. Butch and Joe watched closely. If a fight broke out it might give them an opportunity to turn the tables on the renegades. Suddenly Fakenham laughed.

'Hell, Aaron! This ain't no time to pick a fight. Maybe later you and I can settle our differences. Right now we need to stick together to get away from here afore that goddamn Barca comes back or the wardens from Los Pecos catch up with us.

'OK, Josh, you pick up those guns. Can't leave them behind for these dumb-asses to come chasing after us.'

'Believe me, we will come for you, Fakenham. Every night when you lie down to sleep you'll wonder whether we might be there in the morning, with a gun against that conniving head of yours.'

'Yeah, well if I was you, I'd worry about surviving the next few days when that Barca comes looking for you. Maybe you should start walking now because we're taking the horses.'

'Hell, you can't leave us stranded!'

'That's just what we aim to do. Four horses, four of us. It don't take no store clerk to work that one out. OK, fellas. Load the guns and ammo on the horses and let's vamoose afore someone does turn up.'

Joe and Butch watched helplessly as the horses were unhooked from the wagon and the convicts mounted up.

'*Adios amigos*,' Fakenham called as he rode out at the head of the gang. 'And thanks for springing us.'

Butch and Joe watched the riders disappear with mounting rage and frustration.

'Damn that Fakenham! What a snake in the grass he turned out to be,' Joe fumed. 'Now we're worse off than if we had never gone back for them gophers.'

Joe wandered over to the wagon and peered inside, wondering if anything useful might have been left inside. 'Humph. They left the sack of dynamite behind. Don't suppose none of them knew how to use it.'

'The dynamite?' Suddenly Butch looked hopeful. 'Haul that out and let's have a look. I stashed a couple of spare revolvers along with some knives.'

Carefully Joe emptied the sack. Sure enough nestling in the bottom were two revolvers that looked old but service-able and a couple of wicked-looking Bowie knives.

'Butch, I could kiss you if you

weren't such an ugly cuss.'

'Don't you come near me, Joe Peters, else this Bowie will separate your head from your shoulders. An' ugly ain't the word for you. You're like a grizzly bear as someone had reached up its ass and pulled inside out.'

'What you saying Shilton? That I'm an inside-out asshole?'

'No, I guess that's going a bit too far. I should have more respect for grizzlies and assholes than to compare them with you.'

Lack of sleep, the frustrations and tensions that had built up over the last few days took their toll and Joe swung a roundhouse at Butch that, had it landed, would have seriously damaged him. Butch ducked the blow and punched hard into Joe's belly. His fist sank up to the wrist. With a grunt and a roar, not unlike the grizzly Butch had compared him with, Joe staggered back against the side of wagon.

'Damn you, Shilton! I'm going to tear your arms off and beat you to death,' he roared, pushing his large frame away from the wagon. Then he stopped and stared at something behind Butch.

'Goddamn it, Butch! Just when I thought things couldn't get much worse.'

Butch didn't turn around. 'Nice try, Joe. You won't catch me out with an old trick like that.' Butch flinched as a shot rang out and a bullet splintered the side of the wagon. He swung around and saw what Joe had seen. Both men stared in dismay at the horsemen encircling them. Once more in a short space of time they were held at bay by men with guns levelled at them.

'Ah so, the *gringos* return from the dead,' Barca remarked amicably. 'You have caused me much trouble, my *gringo* friends. This time I make sure you go all the way to the underworld. And I assure you, the passage there will be most painful, most painful indeed.' Then they noticed a familiar face behind Barca. Grinning widely at them was the triumphant face of Fakenham, who was riding along with his three henchmen.

'You will hardly believe our luck,' the escaped convict crowed. 'Just as we were riding out into an uncertain future, we happened to bump into these gentlemen. They seemed mighty interested when we told them who we had left stranded back here. Wasn't that a lucky chance — for us, that is?'

There was nothing the two pals could do. Quickly they were disarmed and their hands bound together. A rope was placed around their necks and fastened to the saddles of two riders.

'I hope you can run, *mis amigos*. If you don't keep up you will be dragged.'

24

'Butch, I say, Butch.'

The response was incoherent, part-way between a grunt and a groan.

'I mean . . . what I mean to say, I'm sorry I took a swipe at you back there at the village. I guess I got a bit mad at you. The awful thing is I can't recall what the hell I was mad about.'

'Joe, can I tell you, that's what got us into all this trouble in the first place. That goddamn temper of yours.'

'What you saying?' Joe's voice had grown tense.

'Goddamn it, Joe, do I have to spell it out for you?'

'Yeah, you goddamn have to spell it out for me!'

'Barbelle, you remember Barbelle? You got in a fight with those cowboys and we landed up in Los Pecos penitentiary. Do I have to say more?'

'You whinging little booger! Why were we on the run in the first place? Who broke the sheriff's Goddamn jaw when he caught you in the barn with Reverend Dinwiddie's daughter?'

'Joe, I'm already tired of this Goddamn argument, so shut the Goddamn hell up!'

'Jeez, Shilton, if I weren't chained to this here wall I'd come over there and kick the living daylights out of you.'

'Yeah, yeah, yeah. I've heard it all before. If you were free and I was still chained up, I'd still whip your fat ass.'

There was a rattle of chains and something like a growl came from out of the darkness.

'For Gawd's sake, Joe, calm down. I'm trying to think of some way of getting us out of this mess. What a snake that Fakenham turned out to be. I wish it had been him as got caught up in that crusher back at the mine. Might have saved us a lot of grief.'

'Yeah, it sure was a bad error of judgement to ever get mixed up with any of them. Fancy us being naive enough to believe you could spring a crook from prison and then expect him to act honourably. What a pair of cow-brains we were.'

'Well, it seemed logical at the time, to recruit more men. And who better to fight a crook than another crook? Now the mob we rescued has joined forces with Barca. Goddamn it, I get mad just thinking about it.'

'Well, think about how we going to get out of here.'

There sounded the rattle of a key in a lock and a door opened, letting in a flare of sunlight. A Mexican appeared at the door, holding a large pistol. He beckoned to someone outside. A woman carrying a tray came inside and placed a bowl of beans and a mug of coffee by each of the prisoners.

'What the hell's happening?' Butch demanded. 'Why are we being held here? I want to see the American consul. You have no right to keep us chained up like this.'

In a couple of quick strides the Mexican guard reached Butch. The prisoner had no chance to dodge the blow as the guard swung hard, catching him on the side of the head with the pistol. Then the Mexican stepped back, hawked, and spat into the bowl of beans that had been placed on the floor.

'The *gringo* will not speak unless I give permission.' The guard gave a curt shake of the head at the woman and she hurriedly left. 'Enjoy your breakfast, *gringo* dog. Next time you speak out of turn, I will piss in your beans.'

'That'll be difficult.' Butch was hurting from the blow with the pistol and was doing his best to keep his voice steady. 'I thought Mexican eunuchs ain't got nothing to piss with.'

This time the Mexican used his boot to kick Butch in the mouth, then he stepped back and aimed the pistol. Butch was spitting out blood, feeling the agony of a split lip.

'You piece of *gringo* dung,' the guard yelled, his voice trembling with anger.

'Only Barca want you alive I would shoot a hole in you right now.'

Suddenly the Mexican paused and a look of cruel pleasure spread across his face. He squatted down on the floor so that he was on a level with the prisoner but out of reach.

'You know why you are still alive, *gringo*? I will tell you. Barca has a special treat reserved for you. Have you heard of the eagle's wings?'

Butch said nothing, just glowered at the Mexican.

'When he returns, Barca will introduce you to the eagle's wings. It is very amusing but very painful for the victims. First, you will be stripped and pegged out on the ground. Toni, a man who is skilled in such work, will peel the flesh on your chest to show off your ribs. He has a special tool and will cut the ribs free. Then everything is folded back like the wings of an eagle and exposing inside the chest. Are you getting the picture, *gringo*?'

'All I'm getting is the smell of pig

dung stinking up my nostrils.'

The Mexican stood up. 'That is how you will die, *gringo*. I will come by as you are lying there with your insides frying in the sun and I shall piss on your heart while you still live. That's what you have to look forward to, *gringo*. It will give me great pleasure to piss on your black *gringo* heart.'

Chuckling loudly the guard departed, slamming the door to and turning the key in the lock.

'Butch,' Joe called, 'you all right?'

'Hell I know.' Butch's mouth was sore, his words indistinct as he spoke and his head ached where the pistol had left a large lump. 'That bastard Mex booted me in the mouth. I think he loosened my teeth.'

'Well, if it's any consolation I ache all over. Hauling us like roped steers back here was one helluva ordeal. I didn't think I was going to make it.'

'That eagle's wing sounds a mite painful. I heard about it afore. Some Indian tribes practise it. They reckon it takes a long time to die. When Barca returns, that's when it starts. I wonder what devil's mission he's on right now? I can't see no hope for us. You reckon this is the end of the trail, pardner?'

'Hell, what does it matter? We ain't stopped running since that damned judge framed us. Since then, it's sure been a lonesome trail, Joe.'

'You know what, Butch, if I get out of here I'm going to settle down on a little farm somewhere. Raise a few pigs and goats and grow a little corn. Sit on my rocker at night and drink my own corn liquor.'

'I tell you one thing, Joe, if there was a devil and I believed in such a thing and he appeared to me, right now, I'm so desperate I'd sell him my soul in exchange for getting me out of this fix. I'd let my soul go cheap too. All I want is a shot at Barca and that goddamn Fakenham and I'd happily go to join up with Beelzebub down there in that Hell place of his.'

Silence fell as they contemplated

their fate. If the guard were to be believed, their ordeal would begin with the return of Barca. The uncertainty of not knowing how long they had to endure before the ominously named ritual of the eagle's wings added to the tension.

But even as he slept Butch dreamed of escape. He had an idea how to accomplish this. Its success was uncertain, but it had to be attempted before the return of Barca.

25

The metallic grating of the key in the lock jerked them awake. In spite of the agony of anticipation and uncertainty as to their fate, exhaustion had taken over and the captives had fallen into an uneasy asleep.

The trek to the outlaws' hideout had been a gruelling ordeal, stumbling along the uneven trail with the rope around their necks, trying to stay upright, knowing that if they fell, they would be dragged until the horses got to their destination.

Though Butch and Joe were fit, strong men it had been an ordeal that had taken its toll on their stamina and strength. Somehow, they had managed to keep on their feet and survive the ordeal, exhausted and coated with sweat and dust.

Barca's hideout was an old abandoned monastery. As soon as they arrived, the captives had been dragged off and incarcerated in an adobe building that might have been used as stables. Metal rings, embedded in the wall, were ideal anchors for the chains used to secure the two prisoners.

Twice a day meals were delivered. The woman who brought the food did not speak and the guard was armed and bad-tempered. The meals never varied; a bowl of beans and a mug of lukewarm, watery coffee.

'*Amigos*, your splendid banquet has arrived. I want you to eat it all up for you must keep up your strength to fly with eagle wings.'

Harshly the Mexican guard laughed as he gloated over his helpless prisoners.

Silently the woman delivered the food, keeping her eyes averted. She had long, unruly, dark hair, a wide sensual mouth and large hoop earrings. Butch noticed bruises on her face.

'I see pig-guts has been beating you again,' Butch observed. 'This woman, who thinks he is a man, is very courageous. He pistol-whips prisoners chained to a wall and now he shows his bravery by beating women. He *mucho hombre*.'

The woman cast a frightened glance at Butch, then hurried across to Joe to deposit his portion of beans beside him.

'*Gringo*, I told you before you do not speak unless I tell you,' roared the Mexican, anxious to impose his dominance over the prisoners in front of the woman.

'Oh, I'm so frightened,' Butch squeaked in a falsetto voice. 'You can pretend I'm a scared female and then you won't soil your pants when you come near. You smell so bad I think maybe you sleep with the pigs. I bet even the hogs turn away when you come near.'

Butch made snorting grunts that sounded uncannily like the animal he was referring to. The pistol was aimed at Butch and the hand holding it was trembling.

'You *gringo* piece of dirt . . . you shut your stinking mouth or a bullet will shut it for you.'

'Oh, has Pedro lost his temper then? I dare you to shoot, you stinking Mex dung-eater. What's Barca going to say when he returns and his prisoners are dead so he gets no pleasure from torturing them. What was that thing you told me about? The hen's ass or something? I guess that's what was done to you, for you look like something that fell out of something's ass. It must have been a mule for your face has taken on the shape of a mule. No wonder the hogs reject you . . . '

'Shut up!' the Mexican screamed and took a step closer.

The woman scuttled out through the door. In a rage, the Mexican guard kicked the bowl of beans resting on the floor in front of Butch and the whole mess landed on his lap.

'Look what you done now you mule-faced oaf,' Butch yelled. 'That's all you're fit for, kicking beans . . . '

189

He got no further for the guard lashed out with his pistol and as had happened with the last assault the weapon caught Butch on the side of the head. Knowing his goading of the guard would in all likelihood bring on this violent response Butch was ready this time; he rolled with the blow and fell over on to his side.

'Oh my goddamn head,' he moaned. 'You cracked my skull. Don't hit me again. Please don't hit me again.'

The sight of Butch, cowering in the dirt, emboldened the guard.

'I'm going to kick the dung out of you, *gringo* trash.'

His boot slammed into Butch's stomach and that was when Butch carried out the second part of his plan.

Almost breathless from the force of the kick, nevertheless his hands streaked out, curled round the Mexican's boot and heaved. The guard, caught unawares, overbalanced and went down. Butch heard the breath go out of the man as he crashed to the dirt. Butch was desperately clawing at the man's legs, pulling him closer. He was at the extreme extent of the chains securing him to the wall. His fingers hooked under the Mexican's gunbelt and, using this as a handle, he hauled his victim closer.

'Come to me, baby,' he grunted.

Butch was immensely strong and his strength paid off now as he bodily hauled the dazed Mexican into his embrace. The Mexican, recovering somewhat, began to fight back and brought his revolver round to point at Butch's face. While he kept one hand hauling on the belt, Butch's other hand streaked out and his fingers closed around the body of the gun.

'Die *gringo*!' the Mexican yelled triumphantly and pulled the trigger.

26

'Aaaagh! Son of a bitch!' Butch yelled as the hammer snapped down on to the soft tissue at the base of his thumb, puncturing the flesh with a sharp stab of pain. It was indeed agonizing but it stopped the hammer from falling on a cartridge and blowing a hole in Butch. At that range the bullet would have smashed through his skull and blown his head apart.

The Mexican was pulling frantically at the pistol in an attempt to recover it from Butch's solid grip. In the struggle for survival some men weaken and collapse as the odds against them appear impossible. Butch had taken on an armed Mexican bandit with nothing but his bare hands. He was also chained to a wall, which limited his movement. It was an impossible task but Butch never contemplated defeat.

Butch put everything into hauling on that gunbelt. While keeping his grip on the pistol, the hammer painfully digging deeper into his hand and the blood flowing from the wound he heaved resolutely on the Mexican's belt.

The bandit was solely intent on freeing the gun from Butch's grip. While hanging on to the weapon with one hand he was now using his other hand to tear at Butch's fingers, clasped tightly on his weapon. He either ignored or did not realize what was happening as Butch concentrated on dragging him close. Butch was still holding on to the gun, but he had another line of attack planned. Judging the moment right, he let go of the belt. His hand snaked out and closed around the Mexican's neck.

As the Mexican felt the fierce grip on his windpipe his head jerked up and he stared at the inflexible face of the man he was fighting. Suddenly the Mexican was afraid. He opened his mouth to shout for help but only a strangled yelp issued from his fast-constricting throat.

With his free hand he grabbed the rigid circlet of flesh and bone that was slowly choking the life from him. Frantically he clawed and kicked his heels as the realization hit him that he was in a parlous life-or-death struggle.

Even as the guard thrashed about he could feel his strength ebbing. In desperation the Mexican let go that rigid hand on his neck and began to sling punches at the face in front of him. He seemed to have forgotten the gun they both clutched. Butch held on grimly, taking a few punches on his face before burying his head in the Mexican's body and taking blows on the top of his skull instead. The punches were painful but nothing the Mexican did was going to dissuade Butch from hanging on to that death grip on the man's neck.

The punches gradually lost their power. The Mexican tried to kick out with his legs, managing to wedge one heel against the wall, but his strength along with his life was ebbing fast.

His eyes were wide open and staring at his assailant. His lips were mouthing words that had no sound, whether curses or prayers only the man slowly being strangled knew.

The Mexican's struggles weakened; the fingers that scrabbled at the hand choking the life from him slackened their efforts and slowly fell away. His mouth was wide open, his lips covered in foam and blood. He had bitten into his tongue during his struggles and the bloody nub protruded as he tried to get air into his lungs.

Butch kept his hold for perhaps longer than necessary, but he had to make sure his tormentor was finished before letting go. Sensing the life go from the Mexican he slowly relaxed his grip. It was only then that he became aware of the gun he was clasping along with the grip of the dead guard. The hammer was still embedded in the flesh of his hand. Cautiously he eased back the metal spigot so that his hand came free. His shoulders sagged and he gave vent to a huge sigh.

During the struggle, Joe could only watch helplessly as his partner fought for both their lives. His own hands were clenched in sympathy with Butch's clutch on the gun and the chokehold that seemed to be turning the odds in his partner's favour. When he saw Butch take possession of the gun he knew the battle had been won.

'Butch, you son of a bitch! You goddamn son of a bitch!' was all he could say.

For moments they stared at each other across the body of the Mexican.

'The keys, Butch; see if you can find the keys and get these goddamn chains off us.'

Butch was stirred back to action.

'Keep an eye on the door,' he ordered.

The bunch of keys was in a pocket and after a few tries the padlocked chains fell away. Clutching the revolver Butch crawled across to Joe. In moments they were both free.

'He only got the one gun?' Joe asked as they stared at the doorway, fearing that at any moment more bandits would pour through and overwhelm them.

'Yeah, but he did have a knife.'

While Joe retrieved the knife Butch stood by the door peering out. To his surprise the woman who delivered the food was standing outside. When she saw Butch her eyes widened in fear and she opened her mouth to yell or scream. Butch reached out quickly and, grabbing her around the neck, pulled her hard to him and pushed his lips against hers. It was all he could think to do to prevent her from calling out. Glued together he stepped back inside and pressed her against the wall. Only then did he release her.

'Please don't scream,' he said breathlessly. 'I won't harm you.'

She did not scream. Indeed all she could do was stare at him in wonderment. Her eyes slid past him and then widened as she saw the body of the guard sprawled in the dirt.

'*Madre de Dios*,' she breathed and crossed herself while muttering an incantation.

'I'm sorry,' Butch murmured, 'I had to do it. Was he your man?'

Immediately a look of loathing appeared on her face.

'Juan? I spit on him. He kill my husband and take me. I am glad you kill him. He is evil man.'

'I'm sorry — I mean about your husband. Can you help us?'

'*Sí, señor*. You wish to escape from this place? Take me with you. I will help you.'

'Whoa there, slow down. I'm not in any position to take care of anyone. When I leave here I'll be running so hard no one will be able to keep up with me.'

A look of disappointment crossed her face.

'Then give me your knife. I will kill myself. That is my only hope of escape from this hell.'

'Jeez! Joe, help me out here. You hear what she says. She wants to kill herself.'

While this conversation was going on Joe was by the door anxiously peering out into the night and wondering if someone might come looking for the dead guard. He motioned Butch forward and they swapped places.

'*Señora*, we need to get away. You can help us by describing the layout of the place and how many men are here.'

A frown creased her forehead as she thought about what he had said. Now that she did not have to cringe before the brutal guard her features were more relaxed and Joe realized she was a very attractive woman.

'I think is ten men.' Her eyes flicked to the dead body and she grimaced. 'No, maybe nine now.'

27

'Nine? I thought Barca had more men than that.'

'*Sí, señor*, but many go with Barca. They plan a big raid. I hear them talk about a train they rob. Barca take all the men for the robbery. He leave not many to look after prisoners.'

Butch had turned around and was staring at Joe.

'*Nine*! Hell Joe, you could take out nine bandits on your lonesome without any help from me.'

Joe turned back to the woman. 'What is your name?'

'Carmen.'

'Listen Carmen, I want you to tell me where the guards are posted, where the exits are and things like that.'

'*Sí, señor*, there are no guard post like you say. They stay inside drinking.'

'You're saying as nobody is out there

on sentry duty?'

She shook her head. 'They drink, and then they go in the prisoners and take the women.'

'Prisoners? I thought when you mentioned prisoners you meant us.'

'No, *señor*, Barca has prisoners, women like me.'

Butch turned around and the two men stared at each other.

'Jeez, Joe, this Barca fella is sure one twisted *hombre*. What you think? We take on these guards and release the prisoners?'

'What? With one lousy revolver and one knife between us and nine of Barca's cut-throats armed to the teeth? Not odds I would favour.'

'Juan, where are you?'

The voice calling from outside startled them. They stiffened and moved further back into the gloom.

'Juan?'

Joe and Butch flattened themselves against the wall.

'What's his name?' Butch asked

Carmen in a whisper.

'Leon,' she hissed back.

'Leon, come quick and see this,' Butch called in what he hoped was an imitation of the dead Mexican.

He pointed to Joe's knife, making stabbing motions. Joe understood. No shooting, to avoid alerting the rest of the guards.

On came Leon, cursing fluently. He was inside the building before he realized something was amiss. Then he saw the shadowy figures waiting for him and he went for his gun.

He had it drawn as Joe punched him hard in the face but even as he went down the gun went off. Then he was lining it up on Joe. Butch fired fractionally faster than the Mexican and the bullet struck him in the head, killing him instantly. The man collapsed, his head spraying blood and brains in the dirt. Quickly Joe grabbed the bandit by the heels, dragged him further inside, then prised the gun from the dead man's hand.

'Sorry, pal, but my need is greater than yours.'

But the damage was done. There would be no surprise now. Those shots would have roused the bandits from their drunken revels. There were hoarse shouts outside and the sound of men running.

'The stables!' someone yelled. 'Where the *gringos* are. The door is open.'

'Juan, where are you?'

'Hold your fire,' Butch tried again to imitate the dead Mexican.

There was an immediate flurry of shots and bullets whistled inside. Joe risked a look around the door and fired at a shadowy figure crouching by a wall. All he achieved was an answering barrage of fire that splintered the door frame and sent bullets ricocheting inside.

'Goddamn! We've roused a whole nest of hornets. What are we going to do for bullets when these six-shooters are empty?'

Butch was kneeling beside the dead Leon.

'We should be OK for a while. This fella has a full bandoleer.'

'Carmen, is there a back way out of here?'

'*Sí, señor*, there is a window.'

'Keep them busy, Joe, while I shimmy out of that window and see if I can flank them. While we sit holed up in here they only have to wait us out until Barca returns with the rest of the gang.'

Quickly they divvied up the ammo. Joe fired out through the doorway, risking getting his arm or hand blown off or a bullet in the head as he exposed himself for long enough to fire a few shots. He had little hope of hitting anything but it was necessary to keep the bandit's' attention on the doorway while Butch escaped out through the back.

Under cover of the gunfire Butch kicked out the rear window and peered into the darkness. Then he pushed his legs through and dropped to the ground.

'Ah, *señor*, you will throw down your

weapon,' a voice said calmly. 'Do not make me kill you. Barca wants that pleasure for himself. I do not want to disappoint him.'

There was little light, which prevented Butch from seeing his opponent. Then the cloud covering the moon began to drift away and slowly moonlight began to expose objects. Butch strained his eyes as he peered into the gloom, trying to discover the bandit's position.

'How do I know you won't shoot me anyway?' Butch asked, hoping to locate his opponent by the sound of the man's reply.

'Don't be foolish, *amigo*. I could have shot you as you came out of the window. Now hurry and do as I say. My finger it is itchy and I am having great difficulty keeping it from squeezing the trigger.'

The cloud cleared at last and moonlight flooded the area. Butch thought he saw the gleam of metal. He hurled himself to the ground, fired, kept rolling and fired again. Bullets streamed out from the bandit's gun, peppering the wall where, moments before, Butch had been standing. Now Butch had the flash of the gunshot by which to see his target and he fired at the shadow outlined behind the bright muzzle flare. Butch kept rolling and reached the corner of the building.

'Damn you, *gringo*! You've killed Giordano,' a voice yelled. 'He was my brother. Now you *will* die and to hell with Barca!'

Butch was reloading quickly. He pushed his pistol round the corner and fired twice more; then, bending low, he raced along the side of the building.

'Another one down,' Butch muttered as he ran. 'That leaves seven.'

28

Joe heard the shots from behind the building and realized that Butch had run into trouble. Perhaps these bandits weren't as drunk as Carmen had assumed. They were obviously shrewd enough to have sent someone around the back of the building to thwart any escape through the window.

'Hell!' he thought, 'I can't stay bottled up in here. That don't help Butch none if he's in trouble. I got to get out there and take the fight to them.' Joe emptied his gun out into the night and tried to spot the position of the muzzle flashes as the bandits replied to his attack. Quickly he reloaded from the bandoleer and jumped outside. Shots splintered the wooden frame of the door and splattered against the adobe wall. Joe dropped to the ground and rolled, holding his fire, and looking for a target. Bullets were kicking up the dirt around him but none hit him.

He saw a dark form rise up as one of the bandits, eager to kill the *gringo*, stood up for a better sight. Joe put two bullets into the foolish man and heard a scream. The hail of bullets around him slackened as his companions ducked back into cover. Joe rolled again and came up with a jerk against a low wall. Quickly he threw himself over the wall; he almost had a heart attack as something scampered away from him. He fired at the movement and heard an animal-like squealing. Then the smell hit him.

'Hogs, by all that's holy!'

On hands and knees he scuttled across the floor of the pig-pen, feeling the muddy squelch of unseen muck beneath him.

'Damn!' he muttered.

But he kept going till he got to the end of the enclosure. All around him animals were squealing and milling around in a panic. Joe peeped over the low wall and saw someone crouching in a doorway. He fired instinctively. The shape jerked upright and Joe fired again. With the second shot the man went over backwards and disappeared from sight. Guns immediately opened up on Joe's position and he ducked back as bullets hit the top of the wall, spinning off into the night.

The hogs were still squealing. Suddenly Joe had an idea of how to get out of the pen. Scanning the enclosure he spotted a break in the wall where a wooden gate was in place. Once more he scuttled crabwise across the mucky floor, this time towards the gate. He kicked it open. Then he set about rounding up the hogs.

Because of the necessity of keeping low, Joe was forced to stay on hands and knees as he crawled through the mess on the floor of the pen. The smell was dire and Joe was coughing and retching.

He moved into the herd of hogs, yelling and waving his pistol. They squealed and snorted and bucked away from this strange creature that smelt like them but acted so strangely. The herd milled around until one of them found the open gate and with a terrified squeal made a bid for freedom.

The unfortunate animal was blasted into a hog's afterlife as the waiting bandits, anticipating Joe's escape, fired a fusillade into the stampeding hogs. But Joe was not among the escaping animals: he was at the other end of the pen noting the flashes of the guns and beginning his own deadly onslaught on the bandits. Carefully taking aim he fired unhurriedly. At least two men went down before the bandits realized their danger and dived for cover.

Joe dropped also and crawled towards the gateway, trying not to think of the mess he was crawling through. The last of the hogs were milling round in panic when Joe joined them and pushed them towards the gap.

Under cover of their breakout he

managed his own escape from the enclosure and he scrambled desperately for shelter. In the confusion generated by the panicked animals no shots came his way and he reached the cover of a building in safety. Then began a deadly game of cat and mouse, as Joe stalked the remaining bandits.

They were keeping their heads down and not risking exposing themselves as they pumped shots into the hog enclosure, where they imagined the *gringo* was still lurking.

To keep them busy Joe took pot shots at the gun flashes, then moved swiftly to another position; eventually he managed to come up behind them. The firing had slackened in intensity and he reckoned it was because the bandits had been thinned out by his shooting. Now all he had to do was mop up the remnants of the resistance and find out what had happened to Butch.

Then there came a sudden flurry of shots. At first Joe thought he had been spotted but no shots appeared to be coming in his direction. He dropped flat and wriggled out from the cover of the building, keeping low to the ground. Up ahead the muzzle flashes gave him an idea of where the bandits were holed up.

He came to a large stone pedestal on which a holy statue stood. He peered from behind this and nearly cried out with pleasure as he saw the crouching forms firing at some imagined target.

Joe wondered whether the panicked hogs were still providing the bandits with target practice. He considered calling out a warning before he started firing, then decided the situation was too serious for giving quarter. Until he knew what had happened to Butch he could not afford to take any chances. He rose up and fired at the crouching figures.

Joe's attack was a complete surprise and the two men slumped forward as his bullets hit home. He dropped behind the statue and loaded his last few bullets. If this went on much longer he would soon be without the means to fight back.

Lying flat, he peered out into the night, trying to spot the last remnants of resistance. For a moment nothing stirred, then a movement beyond the hog enclosure caught his eye and he sent a shot winging in that direction. That brought answering fire and stone splinters splattered Joe's face.

'Goddamn! That was uncalled for,' he muttered.

He risked a peep around the other side of his shelter, but before he could see anything another shot shook chips from the tub.

'Jeez, that was close. That fella's damn good.'

The game of hide and seek was played out for a good few minutes with Joe no closer to hitting his opponent and in fact not quite sure where he was, for the marksman seemed like a will-o-the wisp, appearing and disappearing in different places without Joe spotting his movements.

Joe was down to his last three bullets and was still no nearer finishing his opponent. He knew he had to do something drastic but could come up with nothing that would not risk the certainty of a bullet from his deadly adversary.

A sudden noise drew his attention to his left. He scanned the area anxiously, concerned in case this flanking movement meant that he was exposed. He risked a shot to where he thought the noise had come from but could see nothing to confirm his suspicion.

'Damn!' he muttered. '*Only two bullets left.*'

Then a slight noise behind him made him turn. The hot muzzle of the weapon that had been firing at him pressed against the base of his skull.

'*Amigo*, drop your gun afore your head is blown apart. Phew! What the hell you bathe in, fella? You smell worse than a buffalo's scrotum.'

'Butch?' Joe asked apprehensively. 'Is that you, Butch?'

'Joe! Goddamn it, is that you? What the hell's the idea of shooting at me?'

The gun was removed from Joe's neck and he turned round to glare at his partner, just in time to see another figure loom up behind Butch.

'*Amigo*, I have at last caught up with you. My brother Giordano you left dead. Now is my revenge for Giordano's death. Go to meet your maker.'

Joe had two bullets left. He fired his pistol past Butch and saw him jerk nervously as he did so. At that distance he could not miss his target. The bandit staggered back. Joe used his last bullet and fired a second time at the shadowy shape beyond his partner. The man crashed to the dirt. Butch sank down beside Joe and leaned against the stone.

'Jeez, Joe! That was close.'

'It sure goddamn was. That was my last two bullets.'

'Hell, Joe, my gun is empty. You think there's any of those fellas still out there?'

'Damned if I know. How many did you get?'

'Three, four, I can't remember. You?'

'Probably about the same, I can't hear nothing.'

They listened, and indeed an eerie quiet surrounded the place.

'Come on, we better go see if Carmen is all right. Then go check out those prisoners she was talking about.'

Cautiously they peered out ready to duck back should anyone start shooting. Nothing disturbed the silence of the night and they stood. Butch moved to the body of the man Joe had just shot and retrieved his gun. Still there was no sign of activity. Warily they made their way back to the place where they had been chained up. Joe stepped inside.

'Carmen, are you still there?'

She came out of the shadows and flung herself at Joe taking him completely by surprise.

'Oh, Señor Joe,' she murmured and kissed him passionately. Suddenly he could sense her sniffing. 'Señor Joe, what is that smell?'

'Huh, sorry about that. Fell in with some hogs.'

'Ooouh!' She backed away.

'It'll wear off,' Joe said lamely. He wasn't quite sure, but he thought he could hear someone sniggering. 'We better go see who's left in this place,' he said gruffly.

Carmen led the way up to the main quarters. There was no sign of any opposition as they walked through the courtyard. Once inside, Carmen led the two men to a stairwell leading down into the bowels of the house. Before they descended she lit a lamp and took down a bunch of keys from a peg.

In a dank corridor they saw a wooden door with an iron grille inset. Carmen unlocked the door and Butch and Joe called out, telling the people inside they were free. Blinking and uncertain, the women came out into the corridor until they were all milling around, talking excitedly and thanking their rescuers.

'Everyone upstairs,' Butch yelled. 'We

got to get out of here *pronto* afore Barca returns with his gang. If that happens then we'll be right back down in these cells again.'

There was a rush for the stairs and the freed women quickly climbed to the upper level.

'Right,' Butch held up his hand for attention. 'We're leaving here *pronto*. If you want to find weapons and arm yourselves afore we saddle up that's fine by me. We don't know when Barca is due to return. The sooner we get moving the better.'

29

The village seemed eerily quiet as they rode up and sat their horses, glancing round in some perplexity. Efforts had been made to repair the burned houses but other than that nothing seemed changed except the absence of people.

'Where the hell is everyone?' Joe asked.

'*Buenos dias!*' Butch called out but there was no response.

'Perhaps when they saw us ride up they thought we were bandits and hightailed it into hiding. Don't forget the last time they saw us we were hauled out of here with a noose around our necks. Now we come back riding bandit horses. At a distance how are they to tell the difference.'

Then they noticed the wagon they had taken from the Los Pecos silver mine. A team of docile horses stood harnessed between the shafts as if ready to ferry something or someone back to the silver mine.

'Joe, there's something fishy here. I don't like this one little bit.'

Butch turned to the refugees trailing behind them to warn them to stay where they were when a movement caught his attention. A man stepped out of one of the houses. He had a tight grip on a young boy. A gag kept the kid from calling out. The man held a gun against the youngster's head.

'Matias!' Butch exclaimed.

'Devlin!' Joe grunted as he recognized the brother of the man he had killed.

Instinctively they put their hands to holsters, then paused as more men appeared from other houses, carrying rifles and pointing them at the two riders. Joe and Butch gazed around them.

'Goddamn!'

'Shilton and Peters, we figured you might return here. Just try pulling those irons and first this kid will die and then you'll follow *pronto*.'

'You let the kid go if we do as you say?'

'Sure, just as soon as you shuck those irons.'

For long moments they hesitated, then Butch exhaled noisily.

'We've been in worse situations, Joe. This just means we go back to Los Pecos. I wouldn't want to have the boy's death on my conscience.'

'I guess.'

Slowly they unbuckled gunbelts and let the rigs fall to the dirt.

'Now get off them horses. Real slow and careful. I'm right nervous. I wouldn't want this gun to go off accidental and kill this little fella here.'

Joe and Butch did as they were told. There was no other option. The prison officers closed around in a circle like beasts of prey. Devlin gave Matias a vicious shove and the boy stumbled to his knees. When he pulled the rag from his face they could see the blood on his mouth.

'You bastard, Devlin. He's only a boy. There was no need to abuse him.'

Matias stayed on his knees sobbing.

'It took a lot of persuasion to make him tell us anything. It was only when we started on his mother that he gave in.'

There was a sudden movement in the doorway of the house behind the warder. Joe and Butch stared in horror as a woman appeared, her torn clothes hanging from her body and fresh blood showing.

'Please, give me back my boy. Don't hurt my boy.' The cry was pitiful, filled with distress and pain.

Jubal Devlin laughed. 'Get back in your hovel, whore. He's guilty of giving aid to fugitives. He's heading for the penitentiary. You'll never see him again.'

The woman's animal-like cry of anguish was piteous to hear. As he spoke Devlin had been uncoiling the notorious whip that had flogged men to the brink of death and beyond. Hardly turning round to look he snaked the leather out to strike with an audible crack against the woman's naked stomach. With a scream she fell back inside her home. She went on screaming as she lay inside: the high-pitched keening of pain and desolation.

Another animal-like noise arose. Devlin turned his attention back to the captives but was not quick enough. Like a bear, and with the roaring of that same animal, Joe Peters launched himself across the space that separated him from Jubal Devlin. The prison warder stood no chance as Joe ploughed into him, hurling him to the ground and fastening his hands on his neck.

'You bastard!'

Joe squeezed as Jubal struggled helplessly beneath him, his face reddening and his mouth gaping open as he strove for air.

'You bastard!' Joe roared again. 'I killed your rotten brother and now I'm going to finish you.'

Jubal Devlin, a big and burly man, struggled against that iron grip on his neck. Beneath that attack he was as helpless as had been the little family he had terrorized. Joe Peters had him pinned to the ground and was slowly throttling the life from him.

As soon as he heard that growl from Joe, Butch knew what was going to happen and tensed ready for action. There were six men standing around holding rifles.

Butch did not realize that these men were all members of the Devlin clan. Some worked at the prison and some were overseers in the Los Pecos silver mine. Built like bulls and cruel by nature they thought nothing of beating a prisoner to death for not being quick enough to obey an order, or if they thought he was not working hard enough.

It was against these men that Butch launched his attack. Skilled as he was at fighting, Butch was no match for these brutal men; at least not all six together. Two, three, he might have taken, but six was overly ambitious. They were all hardened brawlers, expert in putting down prison riots and busting heads in mine disputes, and they would not be beaten easily.

The first man grunted and bent over as Butch kicked him in the knee. He straightened up again from an uppercut that Butch brought up from the floor. A rifle smashed into Butch's shoulder with such force that his arm went numb. He whirled and swung out a wild punch, catching his assailant on the side of the head and sucked in a sharp breath as he felt the pain in his hand from the blow. Something hard hit him a brutal blow in the base of his spine.

'Aaagh!' He stumbled forward; feeling his legs weak beneath him, managed to turn and deflect another brutal strike from the rifle with his forearm and grunted again as pain lanced through him.

Even as he went down he managed to hook the legs from under the rifle-wielder but did not see the next man in line as he clubbed him. The rifle hit him in the temple and he saw flashes of lightning. But there was no thunder-storm, only another sickening blow; then he was lying in the dirt, feeling the empty vault of nothingness yawing at him. He went spinning down into that black vacuum, not feeling the rifle butts thudding into his senseless form.

With Butch lying in the dirt, the men were now able to turn their attention to Joe and his stranglehold on their cousin. Jubal Devlin was black in the face; his eyes were wide and starting from their sockets. The prison warder's tongue protruded and he looked to be a goner.

Two of men stepped forward, rifles raised. They wasted no time trying to prise Joe from his victim. The rifles rose and fell, bouncing off Joe's skull, and he was swiftly beaten unconscious.

30

When Jubal Devlin came to he felt as
though a metal rasp had been jammed
into his throat. It had taken several
minutes of effort on the part of his
associates to revive him. For a moment
he could not talk but made his needs
known by pointing to his mouth and
making drinking movements. Someone
produced a flask and he sucked the
life-giving liquor into his bruised throat.
When he had recovered sufficiently he
looked around him and saw the two
bloodied bodies lying near by.

'They dead?' he croaked.

'Nah, but say the word and we'll put
a bullet in their heads.'

Jubal shook his head. 'I don't want it
that easy. They killed Isaac. They have
to pay for that. There's only one way of
retribution and that's the lash.'

The family stood back as Jubal rose

to his feet. He swayed momentarily, then recovered before walking over to the bigger of the two bodies. He proceeded to kick the unconscious man, swearing hoarsely while he did so.

'Like I say, they have to pay.'

He looked around and pointed to a tree. It was the same mesquite the two pals had sat under eating meals when first they came to the village with Matias.

'Take this heap of hog dirt and tie him to that there tree. Strip the clothes from him.'

They grabbed Joe by his boots and dragged him to the tree. Not wasting time undoing his clothing the men hacked everything to shreds with their knives. While this was being done, Jubal picked up his whip from the dust where it had fallen when the big man had attacked him.

'Is it to the death, Jubal?' one man asked eagerly.

Jubal was flexing his arm, allowing the whip to swing back and forth feeling the balance and judging the distance to the naked man.

'What do you think? Folk will have to learn not to mess with the Devlins.'

A large bearded man thick with muscle kicked the comatose Butch.

'What about this one?'

'Toss him in the wagon. I'd better take one back alive. That'll maybe satisfy the governor. Six men go on the run and we don't bring back none alive and it might create some action. I can finish Shilton any time back at Los Pecos. Make his life such a misery he'll be begging to die.'

The warders guffawed as two of them picked up the body of Butch Shilton. He made no sign of awareness as they tossed him into the wagon. Blood was caked in his hair and had run into his ears and down his face. He looked like a man more dead than alive and even his captors were wondering if he would still be alive when they got him back to Los Pecos.

'Hurry it up, Jubal; we ain't supposed

to be this far into Mexico. We'll be in a lot of trouble if the *rurales* arrive and find us here.'

'I ain't hurrying this. An' don't you worry none about no *rurales*. Nobody's interested in a sinkhole like this. Probably don't even know it exists.'

There was a sudden movement and the men swung round to see Matias scurry across the road and back through the door of his home. The boy's mother was still sobbing as she cowered inside.

'Let him go. He served his purpose. See if that thick heap of dung has revived yet. I don't want him to miss out on the pleasure I'll get from teasing him with this here leather.'

One man went to the naked Joe, grabbed a handful of hair and pulled his head up to peer at his face.

'Hell, he's still out.'

The man slapped viciously at Joe's face.

'He ain't dead?' Jubal queried anxiously.

'Naw, he's still breathing. Just plumb out to the world.'

'Get some water. Find a bucket or something and wake him. I'm all fired up. Can't wait to rip that flesh off that fat hog.'

While they waited for the action to begin bottles were retrieved from saddle-bags and passed around, everyone taking long swigs of the potent tequila. Jubal took his share along with the others. The man sent for the water returned carrying a wooden pail with the liquid spilling down the sides. He stood in front of Joe and slung the contents in his face. Joe's body twitched and a low groan emerged. Slowly he lifted his head and stared round vacantly.

'Where the hell am I? What's happening?'

Joe tugged at the ropes that bound him to the tree. There was no give in them. The men who tied the knots were experienced at hogtying prisoners. Huge muscles bulged on arms and shoulders as Joe realized what had happened and strained to free himself. Jubal grinned and the leather flipped out making a neat red mark on Joe's back.

'Aaaagh! Goddamn!' Joe roared.

The men drinking the tequila cheered.

'Bravo Jubal! Strike one for Los Pecos.' Joe tried to twist around to see who his tormentor was.

'I'll kill you!' he roared and the audience of drinkers guffawed loudly.

Again that deadly lash flicked out and took a piece of flesh from Joe's buttock. The big man's body tensed when the pain sliced through him but made a heroic effort to bite down the cry of agony that rose to his throat. The audience waited for his bellow of pain. When the drunken spectators realized there was to be no hollering from the victim they began to berate the man with the whip.

'Hell Jubal, you lost your touch. Let a man at the job. I'll soon make him howl.'

Jubal needed no encouragement but he resisted the temptation to lay the lash on thick. This was a process to be savoured and not hurried. He hit Joe in the shoulder this time and took great pleasure in seeing the body flinch even though his victim made no sound.

The flogging of a man to death is an art. It had to be a long drawn-out process with the victim suffering exquisite pain right up until he expired. Jubal Devlin was an expert in such work. For much of his adult life he had practised on the helpless prisoners of Los Pecos penitentiary. It was as if that training had primed him for this act of revenge as he prepared to flog to death the man who had killed his brother.

Jubal knew he had plenty of time. He knew that by the end of the process Joe's ribs would be exposed as the lash stripped the flesh and his victim would be moaning and begging for mercy.

But there would be no mercy. Only death lay at the end of this process. A long agonizing death that would give much pleasure to the onlookers and none more so than to the man wielding the deadly lash.

31

Butch was swimming up through a dark, viscous fog. An invisible force was holding him back, making his movements slow and arduous. He battled against it, sensing he must escape this gloomy place if he was to survive.

Pain seeped in; brutal numbing pain in his head and in his body. He tried to put his hand up to massage the source of the pain but his hands felt as if they were not part of him. Sudden and fierce agony flooded him and he wanted to flee back down into the darkness, where the pain did not exist but it was too late for that. Now he must endure. Fighting against the throbbing agony he forced his eyes open.

At first he thought he was on a boat. The wooden sides of the wagon puzzled him. He had no memory of rivers or boats. A blue sky with a white-hot sun

235

beamed down on him. He closed his eyes against the glare; that only served to worsen the pain in his head. As well as the agony in his head, his body was consumed by a deep and painful throbbing.

Slowly he became aware of harsh laughter and ribald shouts. He had to concentrate hard as he puzzled over this noise. At first he believed he was back at the outlaws' hideaway and the noise of revelry was that of the bandits returned from their raiding. He tried to roll over and came up against a lumpy object.

For moments he stared at the sack lying in the wagon with him as memory came flooding back. This was the wagon that had carried the convicts from Los Pecos silver mine and this was the sack of dynamite Joe had brought from there. Butch lay back, listening to the sounds around him, trying to ignore the pain that swamped his body as he breathed.

The raucous shouts continued and

he began the slow painful process of raising his pain-racked body so that he could see what went on outside his little wooden world.

He saw them then: the Devlin clan. Painfully, slowly, he raised himself further, his eyes seeking and registering the burly figures of the men who had tracked them to their refuge.

A man was directly in front of him, perspiration running out of his hair and down his back inside his sweat-soaked shirt. The arm was coming back, gripping the handle of a snakelike whip. Butch watched as the whip curled out hitting a lump of raw flesh hanging from a tree.

A beast was being flogged and for some incomprehensible reason it had been tied to a tree. And then the beast moaned and Butch began to suspect it was not a beast at all and the horror flooded in as he realized it was a man hanging there. There was not a space on his back that was not covered in blood and Butch felt sick with horror and could only stare and feel helpless and could think of nothing he could do to save the man hanging in the tree.

Joe Peters: comrade. They had travelled the lonesome trail of owlhoots together, helping each other out of trouble; coming to each other's aid when things got desperate. Never letting go, never giving up on each other. Now, to end like this was so sick and insane and inhuman; Butch felt tears of frustration and rage and let his head fall back on the wooden floor of the wagon.

He knew he was next for the beast treatment. Once Joe succumbed they would haul Butch out of the wagon and strip his clothes from him and then strip his flesh with the whip. The indignity of it was too much. He would not face that. He would cheat the floggers. He would kill himself first.

How to do it? He thought of the things on his person with which he could take his life and despaired. No knife, no gun, no means of self-destruction. In the wagon? Surely something in the wagon would do? Gritting his teeth against the pain he turned his head and began to explore. All the time the terrible ribald laughter went on and more flesh was being stripped from his friend.

He saw the sack once more and looked at it with interest. A length of fuse was tied around the neck. It was easily pulled away and he put his hand inside, feeling the sticks of dynamite. If he could ignite the dynamite the wagon would be blown to smithereens and he along with it, bringing a quick and easy death.

He was pulling the sticks from the bag. Joe had said it needed a fuse.

Butch remembered the men who had ambushed them as they were fleeing Los Pecos. He saw Joe grinning at him, holding up a small cigarillo; he remembered wondering at this, because Joe had never smoked before. Then his mind's eye saw the sparkling fuse and he recalled Joe telling him to jump for the side of the trail.

He had jumped, but that was all he remembered until Joe was shaking him awake.

Then, as he fumbled in the sack, a ready-prepared stick tumbled out on to the floor of the wagon. Butch stared at it.

I light the fuse and I shall die.

He searched his pockets and found his tin of matches. The wagon rocked as something thudded against it. Butch froze, the unstruck match in one hand, the fused stick of dynamite in the other. He saw the back of the man with the whip pressed hard against the wagon, saw the sweat running down out of his hair, heard the heavy breathing.

'Hell Jubal! You're all done in. Let one of us take over.'

'Damnit no! It were my brother he killed. I aim to finish what I started.'

Butch saw the hand come up and pull the collar away from the neck, teasing the wet material from the sweat-soaked skin. He struck the match and held it to the fuse, watched it spark into life, then reached out and slid the stick under the collar and inside the shirt of the sweating man leaning against the side of the wagon. He rolled to the far side of the wagon and put his hands over his ears.

'What the hell . . . ?' Jubal Devlin jerked away from the wagon, reaching behind him in a vain attempt to get to the stinging, burning thing inside his clothing that nipped at his back. 'Goddamn hornet!' he yelled. 'Get this thing away from me.'

His family stumbled forward, laughing raucously.

'Sure thing, Jubal.'

They saw the smoke coming up around Jubal's neck, mingling with the sweat-soaked hair. In their drunken, befuddled state they stared at him, not knowing what to make of this.

'Hell Jubal! You so fired up you set yourself ablaze?'

They hooted and laughed foolishly,

crowding around, slapping at Jubal's shirt as he danced about trying to dislodge the insect gnawing at him.

'Goddamn it, Jubal! That ain't no hornet. That's too big for no hornet. That's a goddamn snake of some kind.'

They whooped with delight at this new discovery.

'Stand still, damnit! You's jumping around like a coyote with a cactus up its ass.'

The explosion when it came rocked the wagon. Butch felt it move on its wheels. The horses between the shafts reared up and only their being tethered prevented them from taking off.

Stuff rained down on Butch. He had his eyes closed and his ears stopped against the detonation he knew was coming. Something thumped against the side of the wagon and fell inside. Slowly he opened his eyes. The disembodied head of Jubal Devlin stared accusingly back at him from the gore-soaked floor.

In spite of his weakened state Butch

242

jerked suddenly upright. Blood was splattered on the side of the wagon. He put his hands out to ward off the staring, accusing eyes of Jubal Devlin and noticed that his hands were covered in blood. Raw lumps of flesh decorated the floor and sides of the wagon along with the blood.

'Jeez Jubal! It was good of you to drop in. I see you got a head start on everybody.'

Butch pulled himself to the side of the wagon and stared out at a scene that resembled that of a battlefield. Headless bodies, limbs, spilled intestines littered the ground. Butch felt nausea rise in him. He steeled himself against the horror, scrambled to the back of the wagon and fell out on to the road.

'Joe,' he croaked.

He had to wade through the gore of the shattered bodies to get to the horror hanging in the tree. Butch stared in anguish at the bloodied torso of his friend.

'Joe, I'm so sorry. Help me someone, help.'

He felt a tugging at his shirt and looked down. Matias was there holding out his big knife. Trembling in every part of his body Butch sawed the ropes until they parted and he was able to lower his pal to the ground.

'I'm so sorry, Joe I was too late to save you.'

The eyes in the bruised and bloody face opened.

'Shilton,' the sound was like a sigh. 'What took you so long . . . ?'

32

'How you coming on, Joe?'

The big man stretched mightily, pushed one arm above his head and massaged his shoulder. He lowered that arm and did the same with the other.

'Butch, I guess I'm healing up fine. There's little or no pain when I move about now.'

'Señor Joe,' a woman's voice called from inside the house, 'you want your coffee now or later?'

'Now please.' Joe smiled contentedly at his partner. 'That Carmen, she sure knows how to pleasure a man.'

'I know, Joe. Since we came back from the dust-up with Barca's gang the females have been more than grateful. I wish I could say the same for the menfolk. They become more and more surly with each day that goes by. I sure wish I knew what was wrong with them.

You'd think they'd be grateful for rescuing their women.'

'Yeah, I did notice they go out of their way to be unhelpful. Maybe jealousy or some such. You still with Dolores, Butch?'

Butch nodded and looked away, staring out at the nearby hills. Here and there grew snaggy mesquite trees or the odd parcel of scrub oaks like obscene growths on the barren and parched earth. At that moment Carmen appeared in the doorway with a tin mug of coffee in her hand.

'*Buenos dias*, Señor Butch. Would you like coffee?'

'Sure thing, Carmen.'

The woman handed the mug to Joe and went back inside, reappearing moments later with another steaming mug.

'I hear Dolores's sister, Magdalene, has moved back in with her,' she said as she delivered the second mug to Butch. 'There is not much room in the house she is sharing with you and Dolores.

How do you manage?'

Butch looked sheepish, shrugged. 'We get by OK. It's not so hard. The sisters are good friends.'

Joe was looking up at his friend, a perplexed look on his face.

'Butch, you never told me you were living with two women.'

'I guess it kind of slipped my mind, what with worrying about you and all,' Butch replied evasively. He sipped his coffee. 'I'm glad you're mending, Joe. Sure had me worried there for a while.'

'That Magdalene.' Carmen made curving movements with her hands. 'She mucha woman. She need good man to take care of her.'

'I guess,' Butch said, plainly made uncomfortable with the direction the conversation was taking. 'I better be getting along. Lots to do. I'm going out to Matias today to give him a hand with his goats. Have to do something to earn my keep.'

'Butch, I know there is a shortage of

247

men in this village because of Barca's depredations, but two sisters!'

'Jeez, Joe, what would you have me do? It's not my house. Anyway, them there women need someone to take care of them.'

Joe started to laugh. 'You son of a gun, Shilton,' he said between chortles. 'You son of a gun. I reckon you're going out in the hills with Matias to get away from the attentions of those two women living with you in that shack.'

'Joe, it ain't nothing like that. I feel I need to do something to earn my keep. I'm not a lazy sumbitch like you, loafing about on your fat ass and having Carmen run her feet off looking after you.'

Carmen put her arm protectively around Joe's shoulders.

'My Joe, he is sick man. You leaf him be, to heal in his own time. When he is better maybe then he go in field and do a leetle work.'

Joe smirked up at his friend. 'What can I do? I'm under doctor's orders

— or Carmen's orders, anyway. I have to wait for a clean bill of health from my nurse afore doing anything.'

He settled back more comfortably in the hammock. Butch had rigged the contraption up from old saddle straps and canvas when Joe was too ill to do anything other than lie face down and have salve applied to the terrible wounds to his damaged back.

'Goatherder,' Joe mused. 'I always figured you for a cowboy.' Joe started to laugh. 'What's the difference between a goatherder and a cowboy?'

Butch shook his head. 'Joe, stop talking in riddles. I don't know what you are talking about.'

'The difference between a goatherder and a cowboy is a pail, you dumbass.'

Joe collapsed in gales of laughter. Butch finished his coffee and contemplated his partner as he lounged in the hammock, shaking like an oversize jellyfish.

'Thanks for the coffee, Carmen,' Butch said, and handed the mug over.

With a quick stride he was at one end of the hammock. The contraption had been fastened to a couple of trees. Butch grabbed the end of the rope and tugged hard. The result was sudden and dramatic.

As the rope unravelled, Joe was tipped unceremoniously to the dirt. The big man gave a startled yell and floundered around like an overturned turtle. Managing to sit up he glared around for his tormentor. Butch was heading for the corral.

'Goddamn you, Shilton!' he roared. 'You come back here so I can punch the living daylights out of you.'

All Joe got in reply was an airy wave from Butch as he forked a horse and rode from the village.

'Goddamn goatherding baboon!'

Joe carried on swearing and yelling abuse until his partner was out of sight. Painfully he got to his feet, Carmen fussing over him and joining in the condemnation of the wannabe goatherder. Her language was even more colourful than Joe's and he looked at her with renewed respect.

'Goddamn it, Carmen! I didn't know females knew stuff like that. Where did you pick up such language?'

Carmen had the grace to blush. She shrugged.

'When Barca's men take me to their hideout I was innocent of such things. I obey my husband and work hard in the fields. But the bandits, they are so rough and dirty and they teach me things I would rather not know. Not like you, my beloved. You are kind and gentle and you treat me with respect. I feel like a woman again, now you are my man.'

Joe looked abashed. 'Woman, I ain't no angel. I done some things I been ashamed of in my time but one thing I never did was to harm no woman or no child.'

'I know you a good man, Joe. I am lucky woman have you rescue me.'

She helped Joe sling the hammock again. With some trepidation the big man eased his bulk back on to the contraption.

'You're a good woman, Carmen. You deserve someone better than a no-account fella on the run from the law.'

'You take it easy, Señor Joe. I know what I deserve and you're man enough for me.'

With a contented sigh Joe closed his eyes while Carmen gently rocked the hammock.

'Hell damnit!' he muttered as he relaxed, 'a fella could sure get used to this way of life.'

In a few moments there came a snoring sound from the hammock. Carmen smiled fondly at the sleeping man and left off rocking. She went back in the house and re-emerged carrying a hoe. With one last look at the man in the hammock she strode out towards the edge of the village. Joe Peters slept on, oblivious to the world around him.

33

Butch Shilton sat on a boulder and idly watched over the little goat herd while Matias stretched out in the shade of a stunted oak tree and dozed. It was that lazy kind of day with the sun beaming down and cooking everything. Earlier Butch had asked Matias what danger there was to his goats that required constant minding,

'Señor Butch, sometimes a cougar will steal down and attack the goats. Goats are easy for a cougar. It is fast and not frightened of anything. Once I had to chase off a cougar.' The boy looked round for something to indicate the size of the beast he had encountered and spied Butch's horse. 'It was the size of a horse.' He spread his hands wide. 'Taller than a man, with teeth as big as my knife.' At this, he took out his large knife, of which he was so proud.

'But Matias was not afraid. I ran at him and shouted. He turned his great eyes towards me. They were as big as melons and yellow with anger. With one bound, Señor Butch, he rush at me. I was too fast for that mighty animal. I jump to one side. I could feel the rough hair on his body as he brushed past me. Then I threw myself on its back. Oh, how he screamed and twisted to get at me. But I hold on and I plunge my knife into his heart. How he scream, but it was a deadly blow. I mortally wounded the beast. It collapsed beneath me.'

Matias sat, nodding his head with satisfaction, as he came to the end of his tale. Butch was doing his best to keep his face straight. 'Matias, if I saw a cougar I would jump on my horse and ride like hell back to the village.'

'There is no need to be afraid, Señor Butch,' Matias said nonchalantly. 'I would protect you.'

'Well, I sure am glad of that.'

As if tired out by his imaginary fight with the big cat, Matias lay back and

254

closed his eyes. Butch sat quietly for a time, thinking about the village and its people and the simple life they led.

'Hell, I'm becoming to feel quite at home here, and Joe seems to have settled down also,' he muttered.

Thoughtfully he took out his revolver and weighed it in his hand staring off into the distance. After all that had happened, he went armed now with twin pistols pouched in low-slung holsters.

'Damnit, life on the run is no life at all,' he mused. 'A fella has always gotta be on the alert and on the move all the time. Sure would be fine to hang up these here irons and settle down somewhere nice an' peaceful.' His face creased in a smirk as another thought struck him. 'Ain't it the damndest thing them sisters bedding down with me. Delores and Magdalene.' For a moment he was lost in dreamy contemplation as he recalled the sisters' charms. 'Hell, I think I'll have a word with Joe about settling down here. A fella could do a lot worse. We got all those horses from the men as were intent on taking us back to Los Pecos. We could trade those for a few head of cattle and start rearing beef.' He looked over the goats grazing contentedly nearby. 'Goats are all right, I suppose, but the real money would be in beef cattle. That was my old job afore trouble set me on the trail of the owlhoot.'

He turned his gaze to the boy dozing contentedly in the shade. A smile crossed his face as he watched the boy, thinking of his account of the slaying of the cougar with his knife.

'He's a good kid. I could make a cowboy of him. Teach him all I know about cows. We would all grow rich together.'

Butch daydreamed and planned and felt content on that hot day while he watched over a small herd of goats.

'Señor Butch, I am hungry. Shall we eat now?'

Butch was dragged back from his romanticizing by the plaintive voice of a needy, ten-year-old boy.

'Ah-huh — you what — what you say?'

'I'm hungry, Señor Butch.'

Matias was sitting up, rubbing his belly with an anguished look on his face.

'You're hungry. Yeah sure, I guess now you mention it I could do with a bite myself. What we got today?'

Matias stopped rubbing his stomach and stared reprovingly at Butch.

'Señor Butch, you know it is your turn to bring food. I brought it yesterday.'

'You did! Are you sure?'

Matias threw his hands up in the air and fell back. He said something sotto voce that Butch could not make out. He heard enough to think there might be an element of swearing involved.

'Matias, I declare I might have heard some rough speech from you, just then. Where did you get to learn such language?'

Butch tried to look stern but when he

glared at his young companion Matias was grinning back at him.

'Señor Butch and Señor Joe, them sons of bitches teach me many such goddamn words. I talk like *gringo*, now.'

'No, goddamnit, no! Them's not words for young'uns to be coming out with. Hell damnit, if that's all you learned from Joe and me then we're pretty goddamn poor teachers.'

'*Si*, Señor Butch, now tell me how we goddamn gonna eat?'

Butch threw his hands in the air in exasperation, opened his mouth as if to continue his scolding then thought better of it and shook his head.

'I've a good mind to put you across my knee and give you a good hiding, you young whippersnapper.'

Matias looked up suddenly, alert to a new word.

'Señor Butch, but what is this whippersnap, you say?'

'Whippersnapper! It's like a . . . let me see . . . um, whippersnapper.' Butch was thinking furiously, not wanting to appear ignorant in front of his young protégé. 'In days long ago when they had young boys who were caught committing some crime, they weren't sure what to do with them. Because they were so young, the judge did not want to send them to prison. Youngsters like that would not last long amongst the rough men in prison.' Butch briefly recalled Los Pecos Penitentiary and shuddered to think how long someone like Matias would last in such an institution. 'So they come up with the idea of punishing them without sending them to prison. Instead they were sent to a whippery. A . . . a whippery is . . . ah . . . a whippery is where they make whips.' Butch was becoming more confident as his imagination fired up. 'Now these young criminals were used to test the whips. Every new whip had to be checked out for snap and so the whip-master would try out the whip on the young criminals. That was their punishment, see. They had to endure the whipping from the newly manufactured whips. And they became known as whippersnappers.'

Butch smiled brightly at Matias, fully confident in the soundness of his explanation.

'I think Señor Butch talk the cow-shit that come out the bull's ass.'

Butch's eyes opened wide. 'You young whippersnapper,' he yelled and made a grab for the youngster.

Matias was expecting such a move and easily eluded Butch.

'Bullshit!' he yelled delightedly as if he had learned a new phrase, then rolled about laughing. 'Goddamn it, we have created a monster,' Butch grumbled.

But Matias's laugher was infectious and he found himself joining in.

34

Outside the house that Butch shared with the two women, Dolores and Magdalene, a group of men were gathered. They were standing out on the road, solemn; not threatening, some scowling, all nervous. The men carried, not weapons but tools; hoes shovels rakes billhooks machetes.

'Looks like some sort of delegation,' Joe muttered. 'I hope it's not more bandits raiding or Indians stealing their women. Seems like this place has one goddamn disaster after another.'

'I reckon you're right, at that,' Joe said. 'It sure looks like some sort of trouble, if you ask me.'

Butch and Joe reined in the horses and tied them up before approaching the knot of men.

'Howdy fellas, you look glum as a bunch of bible-thumpers about to confront the town's harlot,' Joe called out.

The men stared solemnly back at the two men. They shifted uncomfortably, made nervous by some underlying emotion. An elderly man was pushed to the front to stand trembling before Joe and Butch. The two pals looked on, puzzled by this odd behaviour.

'Come on, spit it out, old timer,' Butch said amiably. 'We ain't going to bite the head off you. Though Joe once bit a coyote and he died of blood poison. The coyote that is, not Joe, I mean. But if he gets too close I would begin to worry. Joe's smell is worse than his bite.'

'Butch, would you shut up! The fella might just tell us what's up if you'd let him get a word in edgeways, 'less of course you want to talk the poor old booger to death. If words were dollars then you'd be a very rich man.'

'Señor, you must leave,' the old man suddenly burst out.

Joe and Butch gazed thoughtfully at

the man. He wore dirty cotton pants and a shirt that was too big for his scrawny frame. He had taken off his hat and was twisting it nervously in his hands.

'Leave what . . . where . . . ?'

Butch held out his hands in a helpless gesture. The old man did not look at the two *gringos* but kept his eyes on the ground.

'You must leave here . . . the village . . . '

Joe took off his hat and scratched his head. 'Old man, I don't get your drift. Tell me plain why would we leave?'

'Go from our village, we don't want you here.'

Joe and Butch stood gazing at the old man with dusty clothes, his head bent and twisting his hat to destruction.

'What the hell you saying, old man? I don't understand you.'

At this point the man fell to his knees and began mumbling. A woman shouted from inside the house.

'Señor Butch, keel them all. They are

263

no good scum, afraid of their own shadow.'

'Dolores, what's going on, Dolores? Here, let me through.'

Butch brushed past the old man, but found the men behind the kneeling farmer had formed a barrier and were determined to stop him going further.

'I wanna get in my own damn house,' Butch yelled.

'*Señor*, please, you no live here no more. You must leave.'

Butch stared hard at the man who spoke. He was about the same age as Butch with a heavy moustache. With a sudden movement Butch drew his pistol and held it to the man's head.

'Talk mister and talk fast. Tell me what the hell's going on.'

'You not welcome here no more,' the man spoke in a trembling voice. 'We have meeting. Since you come here, nothing but trouble. Bad men come here because of you. There is fighting. Always fighting. We no like this trouble. We have meeting and decide you go from here. Find some other place to fight.'

Butch slowly lowered his gun. He stared around at the farmers confronting him and Joe. They were nodding and muttering things he could not quite make out. He realized now why they were carrying their tools. On this occasion they were not tools at all, but weapons.

'Son of a bitch, you're ready to fight us, ain't you.'

The crowd of men stared at him, nervous but resolute. Butch still had his gun in his hand. Slowly he pouched the weapon.

'Hell, Joe I don't feel right about this. I can't fight these fellas. They ain't nothing but simple farmers . . . goat herders . . . tillers of the land. Tell me Joe, what we ever produced with the sweat of our brow. Did you ever grow anything? Did you ever plant a row of beans and tend them and water them and watch them grow. Keep the weeds down and chase off the birds. They're standing there with the only weapons they have, and that's the tools they till the land with. Year in year out, in all seasons, they hoke in the dirt and plant and grow their food. Then someone like Barca comes along and takes half of what they grow.'

'Goddamn it, Butch what the hell are you saying?'

'I'm saying as we got no right to be here. We're a couple of saddle bums as is wanted by the law. This here is their land, their village. They have every cause to want us out. We're like . . . we're like . . . we just don't fit in. Oh, yeah, we can bully them and threaten them and make them accept us up to a point. But if we do that we're no better than Barca.'

'Son of a bitch, I was kind of getting used to the settled life.'

'Yeah, me too.'

Joe turned and was walking back to his horse. Butch took one last look at the tightly grouped knot of farmers.

'OK, fellas, you win. We'll go.'

The farmers watched silently as Joe and Butch roped together the horses they had accumulated from the men they had killed. When they had finished they had a sizeable herd of horses.

'At least we don't ride away empty-handed. We got all this here horseflesh to sell.'

'Señor Butch, what are you doing?'

They stopped roping the animals as the small figure of Matias came running up.

'We're leaving, kid. We ain't welcome here no more.'

There were tears in the boy's eyes as he stared up at his hero.

'Take me with you. I do not want you to leave.'

Butch reached out and put his hands on the boy's shoulders.

'Matias, I don't want to leave either. But sometimes things don't work out quite like we expect. I want you to stay here in this village and grow up to be a good man. Some day I'll come riding by here and call in and visit, that I promise. The life I live ain't for no young boy with all his future ahead of him.'

The boy's tears were flowing unchecked. He shook his head but could not speak.

'Ready, Butch,' Joe called.

Matias suddenly hugged Butch.

'I will watch for you, Señor Butch.'

Butch prised the boy loose then swung up in his saddle.

'Move 'em out, Joe.'

They rode out. Neither man looked back; the lawless trail stretching ahead of them.

We do hope that you have enjoyed reading this large print book.

Did you know that all of our titles are available for purchase?

We publish a wide range of high quality large print books including:
Romances, Mysteries, Classics
General Fiction
Non Fiction and Westerns

Special interest titles available in large print are:
The Little Oxford Dictionary
Music Book, Song Book
Hymn Book, Service Book

Also available from us courtesy of Oxford University Press:
Young Readers' Dictionary
(large print edition)
Young Readers' Thesaurus
(large print edition)

For further information or a free brochure, please contact us at:
Ulverscroft Large Print Books Ltd.,
The Green, Bradgate Road, Anstey,
Leicester, LE7 7FU, England.
Tel: (00 44) **0116 236 4325**
Fax: (00 44) **0116 234 0205**

DEVINE'S MISSION

I. J. Parnham

When Lachlan McKinley raids Fairmount Town's bank, the bounty on his head attracts plenty of manhunters — but everyone who goes after him ends up dead. When bounty hunter Jonathon Lynch, Lachlan's stepbrother, joins the hunt, he soon discovers that all is not as it seems, and Lachlan may in fact be innocent. Worse, US Marshal Jake Devine is also after Lachlan. Devine is more likely to destroy the peace than to keep it, so can Jonathon bring the guilty to justice before Devine does his worst?

PERIL ON THE OREGON TRAIL

Billy Hall

Hannah Henford, travelling west aboard a steamer, meets the reticent young Andrew Stevenson, who captures her heart with his bravery when the boat docks and they embark upon the Oregon Trail. Jeremiah Smith, a mysterious and adventurous mountain man, discovers Hannah alone and takes her in search of wild turkeys. She cannot help but be charmed by Jeremiah, but he may not be all that he seems. In Arapaho territory, Andrew will be needed again: in pursuit of Hannah, he will face peril on the Oregon Trail.